MW01504710

LOVE on
Blue Waves

Daniel Gallik

Halo
PUBLISHING
INTERNATIONAL

ISBN: 978-1-61244-772-8
Library of Congress Control Number: 2019911525

Printed in the United States of America

Halo Publishing International
1100 NW Loop 410
Suite 700 - 176
San Antonio, Texas 78213
www.halopublishing.com
contact@halopublishing.com

Contents

Preface by Chuck Yarborough of the Cleveland
Plain Dealer   11

The Energies Of The Universe Are Coruscated   13

We Understand the Universe's History   20

A Galaxy Is Moving Away   31

A Theory Exists Only In A Mind   36

Quantum Mechanics Deals With Love, And Finds
That Love Is A Millionth Of A Millionth Of A
Centimeter Long   43

The Universe Has Infinite Parts Ready For A
Unified Theory   53

Time Can Be Measured More Accurately
Than Inches   60

The Light That Left Jane's Friend, Left Years Ago   65

"God Abhors A Naked Singularity." Roger Penrose   71

Gravity Is A Consequence Of The Fact That
Space/Time Is Not Flat   79

Time Is Slower Than A Large Body--Love Has
Nothing To Do With Time   87

All Galaxies Are Moving Away From Us   95

If You Traveled Around the Universe At The Speed
Of Light, The Journey Would End Before You Got
Back Home   101

In The Past The Distance Between Galaxies Was Zero   106

Quantum Mechanics Are About Randomness   113

Einstein said, "God Does Not Play Dice!"   121

What Matters Is Continuous   129

Love Divides And Multiplies Without Limit   136

A Quark Has An Infinitely Simple Flavor
Produced From All The Colors   139

The Colliding Atoms - Up, Down; Strange,
And Charmed   143

Infinite Density   147

Black Holes Are Not Black   154

Ones Never Escape From A Black Hole   167

We Are All Composed Of Language   174

Ultimate Time Lies Within Ultimate Time   179

The Properties Of The Universe   183

Time, A Property? No, An Arrow   196

The Axes: The Centers Of Rotations   204

Love Will End In A Cosmic State
Of High Order   212

Quanta In Mathematics Show Themselves Occasionally   219

Into The Blue Of The Sky Is A Long Way To Jump   224

This Scene Shows Age, Youth, And Death As Unified   231

Two Can No Longer Hear The Physics Of Life   238

Last Words   251

Jane thought with her heart, "I feel a kind of blue that makes me not wonder whether he will come."

Preface by
Chuck Yarborough of the
Cleveland Plain Dealer

*P*eople have been trying to improve on the love story ever since Adam and Eve. William Shakespeare probably had the best update with "Romeo and Juliet," and really, everything since then has been either derivative or a poor copy.

Cleveland writer Daniel Gallik has thrown his quill into the ring with "Love on the Blue Waves," and it just might be that he's found a way to put a new twist on Ol' Bill's classic tale of love.

Jim and Jane are two Clevelanders who don't even know each other, and yet each knows the other is out there. There are no Capulets and Montague feuds standing in their way, nothing as dramatic as that. Actually, it's something even MORE dramatic: real life.

Gallik's novel features chapters like "Know How The Universe Started," "Galaxies Are Moving Away From Each Other," and "Time Can Be Measured More Accurately Than Inches," headings that Gallik says is a way to "let us understand that the love is like the ultimate science to all of us." A mundane news story about a runaway truck, and the public's fascination with it also figures into the tale, and shows both the silliness of our fascination with such things.

Why? Because in the long run, only love matters, for Jim and Jane and for us. It can survive CNN and it can survive even Death.

Yes, Death. Even Shakespeare knew that to really tell the tale, Mercutio had to die.

The Energies Of The Universe Are Coruscated

*J*im was blue. His old, worn jeans; sweater; socks; his mood were differing hues of the color. Work was over this day. And the color was to become lifting in a quiet way and have multiple, soothing meanings for his life, his love, and his unforeseen death.

The fifty-six-year-old took walks when these times came. Time melted as he put one foot in front of the other making his way down Buckeye Street on the eastside of Cleveland. A full snow had fallen. Late January had brought its usual dark and dreary clouds, and shorter days. As winter slowly proceeded, Jim did not even notice any individual clouds. The sky was all one dull, floating non-color. The time was right for this to have happened. Jane was gone and there was no bringing her back to touch his body, to look into his eyes with that deepness that only she could touch by her faithful heart, and to understand Jim's complex and scattered desires.

The years seemed to be a continuous dream for the man. Love had always been with him, if not in actual truth, in sentences within his hyperactive mind. True, Jane had come late in life, and she left quickly. Yet, she had always been within Jim's heart and quick, perceptive mind.

Jim thought strongly about rituals. First, he told himself that most people do not possess a huge desire for love. He might have to suggest deep, polite discussions to a lady on the corpora of this subject. Jim knew that generally we do not talk about it at all. Second, all humans exhibit sexual desires, but not rituals, which Jim considered a religiously based series of acts. "However," he always said to himself, "when being bitten and stung by the massive events of life, we humans often behave in a series of acts while invoking God. That could, I suppose, become the foundation of my Christian ritual. Maybe even a good ritual through my Savior."

This small man thought that men usually have little on their minds other than getting their genes into the next generation. Men are inherently cold about this. And because of that, this greatly reduced any kind of love happening, and would make the lyrics of any male love song that discusses love between humans, moot. In addition, happily mated females start their nests without their special fellows once their relationship has been consummated. The men are destined to a short life, usually ending with a mass of debris within their psyches. Men tend to get lonelier than females. Yes, Jim thought that he had things figured out.

The previous spring, the warm winds had blown the seeds of the maple tree chaotically around the ground. Jim continued his thoughts: "So, what of the seeds and the wind in that instant?

What will happen in a year? What will happen throughout the rest of time?"

Jim thought all things in our vast universe were equal. Days went by. Seasons passed quickly. Storms brewed. Peaceful, warm days began, and all things were normal and right with the end of this millennium. As the hours passed, the wind died down; the clouds covered the hazy blue sky, and a light rain began to fall. The seeds disappeared into the dark soil. Jim thought, "Why the unnoticed seeds do what they do is anyone's guess, and so, I will keep quiet like the ground and a dying wind and let happen what will happen. I will keep alive, somehow, even in this colder-than-usual winter. Someday, a fresh breeze will silently blow, the seeds will sprout, and I will not gasp as I see new life. I will get down on my knees, look at the fragile root, and my mind will lend a wordless prayer. I will then know what to expect from our old universe. I will expect nothing more."

Always, the silent summer speaks. Jim says, "Why so loudly now?" Jane said to her silent lover, "I had nearly given up on you." Many times, so many times, Jim's silent lover spoke within his mind.

The Purple Martins flit and dive over the waters of Lake Erie. Mosquitoes come; then disappear as the shivers of the night arrive. All the children in the neighborhood play desperately. Their parents take them up to the shore of the great, shallow lake; they watch as the tads' made-up boats drown in the wholesome waters. The wind does not seem to bring the sounds of the chimes in the valley, and Jim says to his quiet lover, "What is the wind, and you will say to me, 'Listen to yourself.'" The lone osprey garrotes the bloody pumpkinseed in its talons as it lifts itself to its heinous nest to eat alone. It's just one of those summers for the ugly bird. In the lone swamp in the old neighborhood, purple loosestrife desiccates much of the life in its own beautiful fashion in a way that no one notices. Jim speaks: "I feel like I should write one of my rare poems and tell you so." Jane argues: "You must learn to sometimes throw away your books." Jim wonders why he loves Jane. Nature in Buckeye is dying every moment that the waters of Lake Erie miles north of the neighborhood expand, slashing over the break walls that protect, precariously, civilization in Cleveland.

"Time is the miser of wishes." Jane ardently explains the meaning of high art within a boring Midwest city vista. Jim goes, "Go ahead with your wisdom. It will eventually end you." Jane flirts; says that her and Jim are at an end. Jim kisses her passionately underneath the old maple at the end of Larchmere Street. A kiss that was as violent as it was loving, sensual as it was ugly, and outright sexy and meaning more than human phrases or human emotions can comprehend. Worried voices are heard through their kiss in a car that is passing by. The quiet in the wind has not asked, will never ask, any questions. The lone snapping turtle in the swamp near the ugly lake almost stands up to stare at Jim's rechargeable flashlight, but then, recovers to go do his cleansing deeds with death in the smelly waters. The day has ended suddenly, and Jim says his goodbyes. And Jane whispers, "You did not have to say that." Jim thinks to himself, "Women!"

In sleep, Jim feels like his deadened head has been swallowed by the turtle. "I am tired of this old turtle eating my proverbial entrails. I want to say something out loud. I love you." Voices breathe way off in the night, and they think. Yet, nothing concrete is heard. Such is endless, unspoken love in our quiet world of hushed remembrances.

The stars make each one of themselves known without the moon present. It is their statement within their world. All the small children of the tightly packed neighborhood are sleeping. Jim feels his heart beating, feels the pulsing, and does not understand it. He is quite happy that he does not understand any of this. The sky seems to yawn. The bright stars are set in their places. Jim knows where he belongs. He belongs in the moment. Jane, at this moment, has too many words locked within her emotions. She is not ready for the love Jim has for her. Jim thinks he is not ready because he possesses too much. His full love is too open at this time and must quiet itself if it is to be desired. Words are too much for this love affair in their brief lives. Sometimes, equations in our history here on earth are unanswered in the silence that looms. However, most of the time, all equations are eventually answered.

Both have a new commandment coming to them. "I give to you; I give to you everything that we love as one another. I love you so that we also love one another. By this, shall we know that we are alive and that we have love, one to another, another towards one? And that our love works with no ill towards anyone. Love will be the fulfilling of our law on the earth and above the earth. And that eventually, if we are patient, our love will be LOVE! ...when we meet, finally meet."

Both knew love was to be the first thing, the most important thing. The only thing. That wholesome, patient love is supreme. Utterances are not difficult to find. Yet, patience is. The eternal love is first given that we become children, then grow. On this ground, the love can then, for the first time, speak of a newness -- the command of brotherly and sisterly love first. Power has been given to us for a love that, in early life, is impossible to understand. Both knew they were lucky and divine at the same time to possess love.

"Let everyone," Jim and Jane thought, "take love deeply to heart, that in the first and the great command of earth the peculiar characteristic of all who truly live is love. And let he and she, and with their whole heart, yield themselves to love and to obey that command." For the right exercise of love, the docile two must take heed of more than one thing about it. The two, deep in their hearts, thought that love arises from the love of all things on and above that which surrounds our earth. That it is endless. That love is spread abroad within our hearts and is a wonderful love. Love becomes the life and the joy of our soul. Out of this fountain of love, our human love works naturally. Jim and Jane knew not to attempt and fulfill the command of this kind of love by themselves. They both thought simultaneously that "we are not in a position to do this by ourselves. But we believe that it will happen naturally." Jane said often to herself and others, "I will love him; I do love him. The feeling will follow me forever. A quiet grace gives me the power to know this." And Jim said the same thing at the same time, and it meant the same to both. They knew this without saying many words to each other. Yes, they knew many things now.

"Ooh," they dreamed, "Love has its measure and rule in the love of the two to become one." They felt it was immense within them. "We shall love one another, as we have loved all, as all is added into the love we will share. The eternal love that works in and around life knows no other law, it will work with power in us what it has harvested. Love must be our deed and our truth. It is not a mere solitary feeling. We must contemplate its glorious image. Let our love be a perfect love; a helpful, self-sacrificing love. We discern more clearly that the whole of our new life is a love of our love. Love is always in our hearts, to open a spring out of which shall stream all our love to all.

A broadcast!

CNN. Helicopter hum.

Reporter on copter. Voice quiet. Hear breathing. Then, voice with hum of huge machine comes on: "This is Joe Taylor roving over El Paso, Texas. We have a semi-tractor trailer rig lose on U.S. 10 Fleeing towards Horizon City, Texas. The state police tell us its speeds are exceeding 100 mph at this time. We are trying to keep up. The citizens of our fine state are worried about the possible destruction. Oh, my god, what is he doing now?" The sound goes dead for a full minute...

We Understand the Universe's History

"I know what occurs when the seed and the ground and the wind and sun mix slowly." A long breath, "…Love." All the words spoken quietly and assuredly.

Every day of his adult life, Jim spoke easily to himself. The hope of love was driven into his character early in his teenage years. This lover of nature felt the ultimate gift that human love gives, but he was, even at an early age, patient enough to wait for it. Dreams of it surrounded his daylight and his evening hours and as he slept, in his dreams.

Women, however, did not come in and out of his life. Love wasn't like the movies. For Jim, love was different. Less concrete. A dream. Jane was there the whole time. She just did not come into Jim's life when he wanted her to. She waited. We, his friends and relatives, were not aware that she was even part of his life. The last chapters of this story might have been a dream. We know it seemed real. But was it totally true? And then again, is anything true?

Jim Jones was your basic human. Born in Akron, and later, lived in Buckeye, a part of Cleveland, and later, much later, died in Akron. Saw that his birthplace turned from a dirty tire town to a clean city of light industry with a vibrant mayor who had graduated with him from his high school many decades ago. The lady he eventually met (or did he, or when?) went through the same moments growing up in Akron on the west side near Fairlawn. Jane Smith's father was a rubber worker; died two years before his retirement from congenital heart problems. Her mother, Jessie, lived a quiet life before the tragedy, and lived an even quieter existence after her husband's death. Silence was sixteen carats and perfectly golden when she passed on in her seventies. Jessie used to say to her only child, Jane, and repeated this often, "You will learn many things, and believe me, ultimate knowledge will come, and you will know where you will go and how long you will be there. Then, and only then, you will know about yourself and what you should expect from the old universe and the life it has given to you, and the death, in which great intelligence will free from you, that will make you feel your soul and smile, smile." Jane did not understand much of her mother's knowledge when she was young.

The ten-year-old did remember, in her own way, the nursery rhyme of Jack and Jill. This is how she learned it from her teachers in the Firestone schools: Jack wanted to do terrible things to Jill. Jill always wished to fly to the moon and write a nice poem about the adventure. When they finally got together, and after many years of haggling, they agreed on a simple task. The result? They both tumbled down into nothing, rolling over the soft ground over and over until their bodies stopped at the foot of the hill. Jill needed an ambulance but died. Jack recovered for a while, then he died, months later. Jane had an odd elementary teacher. Yet, she kept the story quietly in her psyche. The story was not one that was talked about often. Life kind of went that way. All was eventually forgotten. Jane thought, why are you into learning about empty meadows and dumb wells that weren't really needed, yet were up high on a hill, that were probably dry because of poor planning? Jane always wondered why simple tales like these are remembered deep within the recesses of the brain and are always repeated to unsuspecting children. Within Jane's unfathomable brain she quietly knew that the total energy of the world is nothing. She knew that total power lay elsewhere. From all this, she learned to enjoy the earth and never question any happening. Jane loved change, and the seasons, and the calm living in northeast Ohio.

She spoke, "I don't know who penned the phrase, 'It is good to do work, but better still to do your will,' but I love it. Just because a person is involved in a good thing does not mean she is doing what she wants to do. Unfortunately, the difference between will and work can sometimes be very difficult to see. Although these differences may appear subtle, they are, nevertheless, important."

Jim always took time to respond to Jane's ideas, "The basic difference between will and work is that when we are doing will," Jim said, "all is working through our lives to do work. However, when we are doing work, we are acting on our own leading to accomplish a life. In other words, although our work may be for a good reason, we are still doing our own thing."

In her deep communications Jane said, "Instead of saying, 'Please show me what you want me to do next,' I say, 'This is what I am going to do for you. Please help me.' I must limit myself to what efforts I want to be in, not the work you want me to be in. Then, I will give myself the desire to do work."

"Here's a personal story to point out how I feel," Jim said. "'He has blood-poisoning in his finger,' my doctor whispered to my mom. 'He'll have to go to the hospital.' After stepping into another room, the doctor said, 'The vein above his elbow is septic and the infection is moving up toward his shoulder. If it gets past his shoulder, it'll move quickly to his heart and he'll die. We only have about a day to bring the infection under control with medication. I want to be honest with you, there is a good possibility we're going to have to amputate.' My mother was horrified. Many fears crossed her mind as she contemplated her dear, seven-year-old growing up without an arm. She realized, of course, there have been many children who have overcome handicaps more severe than this, but she wanted to spare me all the pain. My mother was not as concerned with the physical limitations as she was with the painful trauma that would follow. She knew how cruel kids at school can be, and she would have given her own arm if it were possible. A battle began to rage within the woman's soul. She felt so helpless. She knew she would not have inner peace until she committed the problem to her life's goals, but she just could not let go. My mother struggled all day and into the night. Finally, sitting in the back of the hospital, she surrendered everything. She committed it all to helping me and was now willing to accept whatever was in her mind. Peace rushed into her soul as she returned to the center of her life. Mom opened her heart and a thought came to her: 'He keeps all his bones; not one of them will be broken.' She began to weep. She now knew I would not lose my arm. Once she was willing to give her all, she gave herself back to me. At the time, I was unaware of the struggle my mother was going through. I am glad she got things squared away without a lengthy battle. I, too, learned something from this experience. Up to this point, I was afraid of doctors. However, a nurse at the hospital graciously helped me over this hurdle. On my first night, she gave me some medicine, and I showed my appreciation by giving it back. Of course, it looked somewhat different when I returned it to her. Furious, the nurse yelled at me, 'Young man, I have a whole gallon of this stuff, and I'll keep giving it to you until you decide to keep it down!' I do not know what made her think it brought me great pleasure to toss my cookies, but I was not about to try to tell her otherwise. Knowing my fear of doctors, she tried to persuade me to cooperate with threats of a shot instead. To her surprise, I jumped at the opportunity to avoid her wrath, and, as a result, I overcame my fear of doctors. I realize the lesson I learned here has little significance, but I thought it would help bring back some of my own childhood memories."

Jane said quietly, "It's easy to get caught up in the zeal of a cure and lose the perspective of priorities. If a case is causing you to neglect the emotional needs of your life, you are doing something that is not within your will. I created a Youth for Christ group in Cleveland for a short period in the 60s. I devoted virtually all my free time to building this youth club. Yet, because I neglected my family, my mom Carol had an emotional breakdown and even contemplated suicide. People tell me I am wrong thinking this way. But I think this is true. Having good priorities not only means having enough time; it also means having enough energy. And always doing the right thing. If our personal lives and families are not glorifying, we have no business seeking another area of work. We must stay in our toils until signs are shown to us.

Both lovers were thinking all at once in their dreams, "Emotional and marital burnout is often the result of unbalanced priorities. No matter how urgent a need seems, you'll be able to meet it if doing so will cause you to greatly take on the needs of yourself or your family. We must realize that we are prone to become overactive in our activities. Thus, we need to guard ourselves against this pitfall. We must always do the right thing with a minimum of work."

A brief history of brief people. Unassumingly quiet, and alone in many ways. Such is love in a massive world. A definition, yes, that is oblique. Yet, can you question it? Jim Jones and Jane Smith did not. Both lived and let it happen. Both knew that sometimes love does not happen. And sometimes it does. Sometimes it fails and sometimes it triumphs over the harsh life of the years on an unregulated earth. Most of the time it is quiet. If you don't try to grasp it, you will never see it. Love is written about many times because no one understands it. Such is humanity. They scream about things they know little about. Things that drive them crazy — they want these things. One is love. The big one is love. True love.

Both knew life was like Diane Arbus photographs. They both had her book of pictures. Black, white, and disturbing. Yet, the love within the blankness came out if you looked into the eyes in the pictures. If you peered into the eyes of Diane Arbus, you saw the love she held. Her itchy frames made you want to look at them, then turn quickly away because you had no reasons attached to them. Sticky art was hard to view. The black and the white produced un-emotion. The faces kept you in touch even though you wished to be alone and happy. More often than be together with all the people and feel their oddness about love.

> *Now, we are back. The TV is working again. The reporter (we have already forgotten his name) speaks in his helicopter voice, "the massive tractor-trailer continues at high speeds east towards horizon city. Now, it has gone across the median strip and is heading into the traffic. Cars coming towards terrible destruction are veering off the highway. This has been going on now for fifteen minutes. We do not know the outcome. We are getting reports that the highway patrol, who, of course are following, have tried to make contact with the driver with their CB radios. We do not have any information that they have made any contact. They do feel the driver is drunk.*

> *Oh my god, the truck is slowing, oh my god, oh my god! It is getting in the correct lane, the one heading east, oh my god, it is getting off the highway, that is Interstate 10, on the off-ramp now, oh my god... A light blue sky is showing itself as the huge vehicle gets off the thruway... Oh, my god!!!...*

Yes, yes, yes! Jane and Jim do love each other. Maybe they do not know it. But love's emotion has entered their lives. It is unified and unreal all at the same time. But it's confusing. Love will not leave. This is the first canon of love's life and their lives. Of course, they do not know this. The second canon is a mathematical principle. First they must construct on a piece a paper a cross, mark it with a "c", let the "c" be its name, let the name indicate the regular-shaped cross, let the four conjunctions be injunctions (two with a concrete intent, two with a congenital intent), and all the above should be contracted and glued to one injunction with a mixed intent by both man and woman.

Both Jane and Jim should take any cross and make it a "c".

In general, the two have not learned that injunctions can become conjunctions if they are contracted by a source that has a degree of colossal power within it. They should also understand that no substitutions can replace any of this jargon. Life needs expressions. Yet, no arrangements make any sense unless rule two is followed. Equivalent arrangements can occur if rule two is allowed, followed, and a lively smile is shown towards it.

The reason both are experiencing restlessness and uncertainty at this time, whether they consciously realize it or not, is for the questioning future. This future is for them, and, because of God, it is devoted to them and what they do. Their evolution will continue. Things are to be, even if unplanned. God makes you feel that, even with great effort, they do not happen when you wish them to happen. And sometimes they don't happen at all. And sometimes they happen, and you did not even know they were going to happen, nor did you want them to happen. There is a vibration that is set within the neighborhood of Buckeye, and consciously or unconsciously, Jim and Jane are responding to a call that comes from an unknown source. God is unknown because no one truly understands the immensity of the power or the why's or when's or even the if's of it all. It is a vibration not only for them, but for the good of all people. Because love is the only true gift that is given to all. Not only for the people, but for the whole future of the beyond of the people.

Jim and Jane are challenging themselves to break free in such a way that society and its dictates will no longer confine them as it has done. This is about both discovering their own love and the kind of affection it will be and their integrity and the realm of infinity that they are approaching. Love is about discovering that they are important and do count. It is about being cooperative with others. Love is about a future without fear. It is about the future of their love. Love.

The time is fast approaching when the dreams will flow because, in the past, Jim and Jane sought the meaning of life inside themselves. The need to understand love has now increased. The need to observe and to measure the act of love has stifled life. Now Jane and Jim are expanding their mortality in their little village outside of Cleveland. There has been a great increase in the communication of love with cultures and societies being brought closer together. There has been an increase in understanding. Yet this coming together has only served to accentuate and beautify the differences man and women enjoy in each other.

Jane and Jim think, "There are those within love who have used their lives to seek and gain trust with others. These, like all good humans taken out of context, have accentuated all the meanings of love. Sometimes, this has been a separation between those who have and those who have not. Sometimes, in fact most of the time, it is a separation between love and everything else, including God himself. This is the cause of all the harmony. It is possible for you to continue love within the society if you wish, while at the same time working towards a magnificently sustainable love, for that alternative lies within your own being. Yes, some experience love but never take love to the next step. Maybe true love is too scary. To be the alternate does not mean dropping out, although there will be those amongst you who will want to do this, for they are driven on by a pioneering spirit to start to set up a love which other people can follow. Yes, let's drive towards the massive depths of the huge heart full of love, love, love."

Both people know, "The greatest raw material, the greatest asset that you have which you can contribute at the moment is your love."

As with the tapestry of love, the quality and the beauty of the whole depends on the purity, the refinement, the lustrous brilliance of the multi-layered, many-colored thread. Only then is it up to the skill of the weaver and the quality of the loom to weave the final product. Have you not seen those cloth materials which shimmer with seemingly different colors as they bend with the wind as you gaze, gaze into the worldly atmosphere of the flowing being of love?

This is your involvement in the evolutionary process of this gift. The groundwork you put in now, the work that you do on yourself, and the manner in which you work together with others is what is going to count in the love you make in this world. Only quality lives have the endurance to last through time. Yet they flower through the expanse of love.

God mysteriously said to Jim and Jane, "What you are embarking on is an imperfect process that leads to perfection, but the answer to those questions are very simple. You will be alive. Not the partaking of life that is the present definition of alive, but you will be alive in the sense that you will be filled with sweetness. There will be no need for you to do anything, because you will have no needs. You will continue to be and enjoy love, not wanting anything or needing for anything, while all of the time discovering the greatness of you and sharing your discovery and your greatness with all around you because that is something you will want to do. In that experience, you will have discovered the real purpose of why you are here on earth and that it differs from the preconceptions that you have now, the definitions that have been taught to you by society. Once you have been to the top, you will want to stay there and never fall. Then you will realize that you never will fall, never. Height will be all the time. And you will feel humble, and you will cry, and the tears will be perfect tears because they are from joy. You will realize joy is not a job. And that it is beyond real on this earth, and the job surrounds the earth, and if you gaze out through its atmosphere, you will feel the peace of the galaxies."

A Galaxy Is Moving Away

*T*he gray morning was filtering away as the hours proceeded. A dangling blue was approaching the horizon in the west. A single clarity was in the future. It was a typical weekday wakeup. Shower, shave, the combing of the hair, the straightening of the four-in-hand knot on his tie, and the entering of a car to get to work. To work, and then to leave, and find freedom somehow that night. Nothing new was coming. Yet.

Dreams had been ceasing in Jim's nights. Winters in northeast Ohio usually bring this kind of dullness. A heavy overcast most days. Once or twice in a month, the sun does shine, briefly, then pushes back behind the ever-present clouds.

This morning Jim felt a lull. His mind was not in order, even after a strong, hot shower and a cup of instant coffee. Jim found himself going to his new VCR and setting it to tape on a cheap video cassette Channel 4, CNN, for a few hours during his day at work. While his hands and part of his mind were doing this, a large part of his psyche was reliving dreams he had had about Jane and love, and her face, and full love, and the delicate nature of her long, supple fingers, and good love, and her endless legs, and sweet love, and the way she allowed her hair to flow over her shoulders, and simple love. Dreams were adding to dreams. Love was adding up in a man who needed it. During these times, Jim also remembered the tough times with the lady. The arguments; the continual arguments about where human life was flowing. Jim, like most men, did not fully comprehend all the details. He did not understand his love was born in Akron, like himself, and that she was now living in Buckeye, in the same neighborhood he was living. In a similar apartment. And that work was also not important to Jane. That it was a way to make money in a free, capitalistic society and that was it. Work was not a calling to this woman.

On the way to work, Jim was shivering. He could not warm up. Fingers grasped at the controls, but it seemed like his car was not gaining any heat. On I-480, the car on autopilot, Jim was feeling emotions. The ones men do not desire. His eyes watering, a crying in a quiet way came. Jim looked deep. He was worrying that Jane was leaving him. Flight was coming into his heart. Like, he was feeling that she was withdrawing because he had too much to deal with in the complicated life of the two thousands. Being alone was easier to Jane at that moment.

Jim was crying so loud, his noise was heard over the tape machine in his car, playing James Taylor and his acoustic form of city folk tales. Jim began to plead, "Everything will be fine. I will get better. I will be someone good to love. I will. Jane will stay with me."

Yet, the negative feelings continued throughout the day. Lunch went badly. Jim's boss stopped by his desk to explain to him that he wanted Jim to be more productive and less into smiling during his days on the job.

After lunch, for once, Jim did not think about his boss and his quotes. Jim's soul quieted. The chaos of the routine business life was going quiet. Jim felt more in control. His emotions were ceasing within his fault line and his mind was starting to see the light of his love for Jane. That there was always a way. A way to experience the beauty in life when love enters. Jim was seeing, that if he was patient, love would come, and all things would be fine.

This is CNN! The story continues. This man in this huge Kenworth tractor-trailer continues his journey to nowhere. No deaths yet. When will it happen? To this newsman, it is inevitable that death will come; to the man driving this huge vehicle or an innocent passerby or another driver in another vehicle. We will continue bringing you this story until it ends. And now a message from our sponsors... but wait, something is happening... he is missing other cars now that he is on a minor route, heading back toward El Paso on Route 62/180 West... Oh God, what will happen... God only knows what will happen... as this man and his massive truck head back towards El Paso on Route 62/180... what will happen here in Texas... (a quick commercial flits on the screen).

Jim did not notice that he had set his VCR. Events at work were dissolving as he entered his kitchen to create a dinner for himself. The man liked his cooking. He could create meals that were tasty, simple, and did not add weight to his aging body. His stroll through his kitchen was becoming automatic. More time for his mind and heart to be in love with Jane, and her ever-present comings and goings, and stayings for periods of time. And her love for him could be tasted, tasted on Jim's tongue like his evening meals. They were warm, and fit well, and meant more than anything in his dismal Midwest life.

Jane's universe was now stable, not moving. Jim was happy over small things. His mind pushed and pushed, and this day, after a hellish falling into chaos, was coming back to the fact that the lady was indeed going to be pushing into Jim's life on this wandering earth.

Ah... Jim was feeling this short word in his heart. Ah kept dashing into his mouth. The tiny syllable was making Jim feel like life was worth the while. Jim was starting to feel life was not work but waiting. Patience, never a virtue in the man, was beginning to show itself in his deep lust for love and it was making him feel fine. It was getting to be fine to wait, hope, and understand the prevailing time.

Wait a moment... This is your correspondent. This, again, is Joe Taylor, reporting the breaking news from near El Paso, Texas... An hour ago, a massive tractor-trailer was hijacked by a suspect, a male suspect, as it sat idling in a truck stop near here. The law breaker commenced to drive the huge vehicle east, out of El Paso towards Horizon City in Texas. A few miles out, the driver changed the colossal vehicle and drove it into oncoming traffic in the west lane. Luckily, and this reporter emphasizes, luckily, he did not hit anyone...and then, the criminal headed off the limited access highway, and drove it west, back towards El Paso, on 82/180. Our copter pilot is getting tired, yet, we proceed, watching the drama unfold and waiting for death to come... Oh, my god, here he goes, sidestepping parked cars, twisting and turning his truck, missing dogs, bikers, and other non-suspecting citizens going and coming from work... Oh, my God, more and more...driving west...soon to be getting back to El Paso and the thousands of people that live near this four lane street outside of the city....we will cut back to the desk and Jack will give you the headlines in today's news...

Mathematically, things evolve. Love is not in this subject. Or is it? The equation X squared plus one equals zero. Solve it and you will find it cannot be solved. Math nuts call all these kinds of numbers imaginary. Funny way to define something they cannot find the answer to. They will say, "But you cannot find the square roots of negative numbers."

Others will think, "Ah, then math has parts that are other-worldly, and as unreal as infinity."

One should allow a barb in these kinds of signs to indicate the direction of changes. Will Jim and Jane find each other? Most mathematicians will tell you that they already have. They just do not know it yet. Odd what words in every discipline can do to explain what love should be about.

Jim should suppose that the value of any arrangement should be the value of a simple expression to which, by taking steps, love can be changed.

A Theory Exists
Only In A Mind

*J*im awoke again; no dreams the previous dull night.
Same weather. Many days and nights happened to this
man; all were the same. No disturbances. Nothing. A dead quiet.
The usual.

The days were dead on. Yes, the three S's began them. Shit,
shave, and shower. Get to work, get to work within his brain, do
your job, come home and relax. A definition to Jim's life was a
waste of time. All of us live like this. None of us are willing to
admit it. Jim thought these thoughts. He knew he was like every
other man in this quiet world. And it did not bother him.

The Diane Arbus photos kept collecting in his mind as he
drove to work. Twins, a lot of twins with funny faces and eyes
that seemed to be pointing in odd directions. The same clothes
on (parents are into doing these things even when the children
are barely out of the womb). And the sex pictures, jilted women
in whorehouses pumping odd lives out of their eyes and aiming
those lives and eyes at you, an innocent bystander who wanted
to be strange, too, but did not have the guts to be that strange.

All the photos. And what was the detail Jim was remembering? Something about Arbus' husband or father or something like that being on the old reruns of M.A.S.H, the TV version with Alan Alda, yes, the doctor or something, the psychologist in the army who treated weirdoes who were caught in war. Anyone knows who watches that strange half hour show that keeps being shown, shown forever on a TV that has seventy channels and a million commercials going on at one time on your set, your TV set. All this stuff happening as a man drives to work on autopilot to make money trying to do nothing and not get caught by his boss, who seemingly cares. A man who cares if work is done. An eerie job in life. An eerie life. But, hey, everything is fine. Everything is OKAY! Honest.

Then, Jim is going to exit. Suddenly, he remembers he had an older brother who died at birth. Still born. His mom used to talk to him about this happening in her life. She said to Jim, "I remember Bill."

"I remember Bill well."

"I mean, I carried you well. You would rumble around in my stomach, like you were a gymnast, and your dad thought that was funny. That we would be raising a gymnast along with your older sister."

"Then, in the ninth month, his activity ceased."

"I don't know what happened."

"I didn't tell your dad."

"That was the only mistake I made. I think."

"Then, one morning, I get tired of thinking about it. I caught the morning bus while dad was at work and went to the hospital."

"And they immediately told me he was dead. They said he. The word he."

"I cried at the hospital. Of course, a lot of people cry at hospitals. No big deal. The doctor said this happens all the time. People die. When they are young, when they are adolescents, when they are middle-aged, and when they are old. We're sorry Ma'am."

"I mean, I thought I would tell you that. I don't know why I am telling you that. But I am."

"So there, I said it."

"Your older brother is dead. He did not have much of a life."

"And, he is dead. He is dead." And then, she always cried. And I looked at her and didn't know what to say to the only woman I would ever feel at total peace with until I met Jane.

The elevator that led to work had a horrible hum, like it should be fixed. No one cared enough to tell anyone or to share with anyone the noise. They just wanted to get to work. Work, and then, go home, down that humming elevator to cars and back home and sit out the winter in northeast Ohio in a warm house watching TV and napping, and watching TV.

This is CNN...We have a development in the story of the man who stole a sixteen-wheel tractor trailer in el Paso, Texas two hours ago...This is Joe Taylor reporting...

We have the video... we will be getting back to our live broadcast in a moment... watch this... yes, the driver is heading west on a four-lane street possibly back to El Paso... here it comes... A pedestrian, a boy who is probably skipping school today, is riding his bicycle along the highway... watch... here it is, wow... look... wow, the driver in the massive truck, the Kenworth, almost hits the kid... wow now we are back to our live shot, we who are up in the TV 8 copter... and he is still at it.... driving his stolen truck back to town... what will happen, next, wow, what will happen to this man and his huge vehicle and the innocent citizens of the El Paso area? Wow.... and now back to CNN for more major news stories... the national and international news.... wow!

Jim knows the inaccuracies, the meanderings, and the complexities of worlds that enter his head.

What Jim needs is love. His brain is entered again, this time with good thoughts, love, and the wishes to find happiness in cycles that enter time and make it become a huge, wonderful investment.

Jane comes to his front door and says hi. Jim lets her enter and have a seat, and he gets her refreshments and tries to start over with her. They need a good start this time. No arguments about deep events in life. Love. Let love blossom.

The sweetly hermetic, golden flower. She blooms, keeps blooming over a whole life. Beauty. Her naturalness has no mind, her ways have no name. She is a visible essence, her sky and light are tender leaves, her two eyes complete her soul. God knows her and gives her to Jim, and he accepts, and is delicate with her, and alive with her, and they find out that time is eternal; they will die and become one in eternity, and verbally they begin to not talk as much and live on as one and are happy as happy ever can be. Extremes are reached, and they are okay, and fine, and have nothing really to worry over. They cultivate reality and obtain essence, and reach an absolute unity that is love and will be love and will last forever and ever, and all those esoteric terms that mean nothing to non-lovers, as life rolls over and over. The golden flower lives, one light, the beauties and beatitudes of heaven, the highest heaven because they have obtained love somehow, and that is the way all things are in our big life, and they are sorry others have not obtained it, the big It, the most sublime realm, the hearts, the one heart, the original face of love, the love, their love, no swords except in everyday life like buying groceries... And Jim's mind ends these moments in realities of life, and everything seems to be fine even though it is not. No problems he ever runs into can take away the gift of love from him. He is fine as a lover. He likes everything. He knows he has love now and will see total love when God will give it to him, and that Jane and him will be forever. How can you be upset at your boss giving you extra work if you already possess the superior gift of love?

Jim goes shopping.

A liquid blue enters his soul, and the shopping goes well. Jim is back at life with his dreams surrounding him. Jim was never a good shopper, an economical shopper, but he was a happy one. Not many groceries to buy anyway. One person, a one-thing-at-a-time person. Not much food needed to live. Not many things needed to live.

At this moment Jim and Jane had a small hopeful love.

Winter and the wind. And feelings of death. Jim, like so many of us, dreams, at times, about committing suicide.

"I am alone. This only happens when I am alone."

"I have a wish to walk to the opposite hillside."

"This hillside climbs like a massif. Huge, and its weight brings fear into me. I hate fear. I want to be away from all this. But something in our spirits attracts us to this. This massif."

"The hillside has brown outcroppings and it appears dangerous to common ones."

"The whole scene exposes the worst parts of winter. The demons that exist within winter, that quietly scream at you and try to keep you away."

"A greasy kind of winter penetrates the valley you are now looking into. You have climbed to another hill, a safer hill. But you are still looking, peering at the massif."

"The river's axle is running in a direction I do not know."

"You begin reading upward this usual winter's brown and gray tints. You do not feel alive already. A dullness has come to you to make you feel unafraid of death. You somehow know all of this is wrong."

"Then, off in the distance on the hillside, you spot a singular red pine tree greening the sad and dead colors that surround the frost, and you wish to be under it. You hope the pine's proven boughs will protect you against all your bad dreams."

"A wind rushes up the incline."

"Flakes of snow assuage the deep clouds. A harsh front has collided with parts of your ugly life."

"A scary vagrancy creeps around in disarray."

"You hear an odd whistling along the hard ground."

"You suddenly feel a push."

"You want to get there."

"But you think about your wishes to meet Jane. You know if you try, you will get to her. Love takes you away from death. Love is not connected to this kind of death. You say, 'I will get there.' And the nightmare is forgotten and death dies..."

Quantum Mechanics Deals With Love, And Finds That Love Is A Millionth Of A Millionth Of A Centimeter Long

"I am alone. I listen. I hear the beating of my own heart. Still, there is another. Another heart." Another morning. The wake up is the same. The flow, the current of life is ever onward. In a commoner, the human heart, the face of it, is never truly pitied. This happens because there is no place in the universe that does not have calamities. The sorrow is deep and quiet, and meant to be suffered alone.

Yes, but love is there if the place is earth. But most of the time, the gift is quiet and not appreciated because it is shaded by the desperate adventures of the pushes of going and doing hundreds of things in one day. Jim feels dozens of weights pulling all the time. Most of the time, days are not good for him. Jim is getting older. He wishes to cry but he has learned that that does no good. The tears do not help anything other than to expulse the sadness out into the public air. That still does no good. Physics teaches that there is an odd equality as far as energy and matter on the globe is concerned. Sadness leaves. Sadness will come back. Jim remembers the news story years ago when Walter Cronkite was doing the CBS national news. A lady standing outside her farm in Kentucky was crying. The newsman asked her how she felt about the Tennessee Valley Authority damming the river near her home, and how the valley was filling with water forming another lake in her district. Her sad face wished to cry. Yet, her eyes welled with tears like the dam that was forming an impoundment. Fresh, lively trees were losing their height and their lives because the water was creeping up their trunks. The slow process made the pain continue in this older woman's face for years to come. She could not express herself in words. She would not express her grief. Still, the reporter tried to dig the truth from her. Her eyes were telling the full story. He did not recognize this. He desperately desired words.

The dreamer remained in Jim. Jim remembered an Einstein quote. Mr. Einstein was his hero because of the things he said, not the science he discovered. "To know that which is impenetrable to us really exists, manifesting itself as the highest wisdom and the most radiant beauty." To Jim, the beauty was love. He interpreted that love was coming towards him. The moments it remained aloof was the mystery. Jim knew that time was out of his scope. He knew a young, wonderful tree would grow out of his ruins. Love would be the tree. Deep inside he also knew the tree would eventually die on this earth. Yet, it would go on within him through eternity. Jim knew his heart was as restless, turbulent, and strong, and as difficult to subdue as the huge tree of life. Wonderful life, love, was speaking to Jim every day now. He needed to be patient. It was coming. Deep love with roots deep into the cosmos. A wonderful time was arriving oh so slowly.

Love. So, yes, Jim always pushed through his sadness. He knew he needed to crash right through it, and smile.

Jim tried to speak to himself when he got low, "I am, I am alive...,I am a hunter...,I am a man..., I build..., I know the type of wood that is in life..., I hunt for the good wood..., I am an artist..., I am..., I will find love when it approaches me..., I am..., I will throw away myself and find her..., Jane is there..., I know she is there and will come when she is ready..."

Life's street came into Jim's view walking to work from his car. The usual walk, yes, full of love, but also other images that he was seeing, and some of those vivid pictures disturbed him, but still, did not get beyond the love he was holding for the future. The images were like family photos' brown and torn edges. They were too old to take deep within him. But they were there. The old man with the huge mustache looking for money with dead trees was behind him. One woman staring ahead, waiting desperately for the Cleveland Transit train far ahead and viewing its slow stops to pick up the morning commute. The leaning shadows from the buildings came upon the ever-live visages. Yes, there were white people in Cleveland who from a distance looked Black. Black people who looked white. Who acted white. Who acted rich. And sounded like white people. And laughed in the subdued way successful businessmen laugh. A young boy Jumping across a puddle and not having enough ability to clear it and splashing the dirty water with his new shoes and giggling about it all. A drunk sleeping on a warming grate down on E. 9th Street, not hearing the noise of the busy Monday morning and its headaches, but still, having a grand headache of his own. A retired mom and vacationing father with sad faces waiting for a bus to get out of town, and then, they would be happy. A little girl looking up into the sky beside a building whose paint was falling off its sides; you could see flakes of it lying on the sidewalk. A nosey pedestrian gazing through a hole in the plywood of a closure hiding the new renewal work on another older building that was in the town. An entirely fat man Just sitting there like a mountain. The puzzles of a woman selling hot dogs to pedestrians during the early morning hours. Dirt and litter and chaos. A man lying nude in the small park across the street. Another man who had the appearance in his eyes that he may be armed. One woman, older, selling paintings of plums. One lady looking like a prostitute but not saying a word. A gay man acting his act, and gasping. He Just missed his bus. And now was crying. A recognizable newsman walking to work; not looking like he cared to see any of the stories present. The sexy legs under a miniskirt. The flowers, fresh and true, inside of a florist's shop. A cat. A boy going to school, with his coat tugged over his head because he owned no hat. A fishing boat way out on Lake Erie even though it was winter. A little girl, obviously not going to school, with two bottles of wine within her grasp and traveling fast down the street. One dead tree, dry and brittle in a planter in front of the florist's shop. A thoroughly white guy with white paint all over his clothes going to work as a painter. One couple, lovers, arm in arm, gazing into one another's eyes, and smiling. Two beggars sitting in the prone position outside of the First National Bank. An old woman with a flag pin on her large lapel, waiting for her bus. A drunkard sleeping on a bench. A priest walking briskly. A fat man with an ice cream cone going to work with his suit coat stained. An Indian crying. An artist carrying his painting into another gray banking tower. The sound of a train way off. Grizzled hums (origins unknown). The sky was entirely blue this winter morning. A dog barking as if frightened by someone or everything. Few laughing. Another crying. Another moment and everything would change. And nearly the same phrases could be written. Jim had a lot going on, and love. This man tried desperately to emphasize love. And he succeeded.

Two women were talking in the Otis elevator that headed up as Jim approached his job. They were pretty and narrow. One said, "What was the price?"

The other said, "Don't worry. My femininity is superb."

And the other said more. The words were spewing, "You feel like a magician, don't you?"

"Only 300 dollars."

"This can mean, you want to wear it for kicks."

"Ah, you, and all your eggs. You are just a hen. And pretty, too."

"Yes, and this weekend he took me to a hotel, a getaway weekend thing."

"You can't come on strong. They feel so, I mean, so threatened."

"All this good stuff happens to you because you dress for yourself."

'Right."

'That is so sweet of me."

"He loves you when you sing to the music.'

"Yes.'

"Sometimes your femininity bugs him."

"Yes, but he loves me more."

"Terrific."

"Okay, so, you were left alone with him. Then, what happened? Nothing, as usual."

"Nothing."

"He doesn't know? He doesn't? Is it a game he likes to play?"

"Yes."

"He is like an old song, isn't he? A plain, old song. Dull and good, and one, at this time of your life, you hear well?

"Yes, you are totally correct so far."

"Are you going to get fired over this?"

"No, my boss does not care. And, even if he does, he will blame it on him."

"You will laugh, and he will cry?"

"Such."

The elevator stops at the twentieth floor. No one gets out. The conversation goes on like it has never stopped.

"He will be your last one?"

"Maybe."

"Hope so?"

"Yes, getting tired of wearing my tight clothes."

"We ladies can be very nasty. Ha, ha."

"It is fun."

"Yes."

"But I keep thinking we are ants."

"But they are powerful."

"Ha, ha."

"Let's straighten it up now."

The two get off. Jim travels to the thirty-seventh floor, gets off, and goes to work. Eight hours later, he leaves.

Love is within his heart as soon as he gets into his car. Jim feels it and the words that go with it. He keeps thinking of the names Jim and Jane, Jim and Jane, Jim and Jane. The higher soul is where love is concealed then revealed when it needs to be felt. Love resides within the eyes. During the day and at night it is within the heart, then it awakes in the morning under the hot shower and goes back into the eyes. Love lives with Jim's dreams.

The conscious mind controls everything else and does a good job of it. The heart controls love, and mess entails. Jim learned to live with that. At times, when he is in a good mood, mess even seems funny.

Jim learned to keep to the chamber of love's origin. The wonder of the heart began to become the reason why he lived. The fire, with his love, illuminated his eyes. The fire of its spirit made him function with a lust of being. All his consciousness began to feel the freedom of flying into the future. Jim's vitality was full. The embryo within this sage's hood was developing like he was becoming a deep philosopher, but a philosopher that was only needed within himself. The light had been turned to on. Jim's darkness was now only becoming a curiosity. Huge dreams livened him.

Jim knew that the love he would find with Jane would turn into a vision that was a celestial kind of mind. Yes, it would go from the heart and form its own wonderful vision and go deep into the fibers of his brain, its own mind. And as more time passed, this love would be truly timeless. No more worries about opaque things, the density of living in Cleveland, and the forms of food and breaths and bodies.

The higher love liked life but did not need it.

The turning of God's light would bring a lasting pleasure to the finiteness of time on earth. Jim was saying, without knowing it, "Oh Jesus, Oh!" And he kept saying it without understanding what he was saying, or even hearing it.

This is Joe Tayler again... The big truck is moving, and things are worsening...we are hearing that most folks in El Paso know about this accident waiting to happen...

we observe that more emergency vehicles are out on the streets trying to prevent the worst from occurring. I do notice them...now, oh my God, pow, I mean, pow, he hits his first vehicle with the eighteen-wheeler... oh my God, and the bicycle is thrown all the way across the four-lane highway, that is Route 62/180, and I see the delinquent child crying on the street.... this is terrible... and now back to the desk, and Jim Jones, who has the morning headlines for you... we will be back with more tales of this accident waiting to happen....

The value of an arrangement, no matter how mathematical it is, is good and true, and if computed correctly, is good for the earth and good for life, and good for goodness' sake. No need to simplify terms. No need to cancel or to condense. The simple expression, all valued in numbers, is a hypothesis that is all about love, and all equals one. All equations solved equal one. All arrangements need to be simplified. One needs to take the time, and one will find out they all equal one. The canons need to be known. But once they are learned, the learning needs to cease. The one sees love. One is one then, and happiness, true happiness will reign without war. Time will stand still in those moments.

All simple expressions lead to love.

Bohr, Einstein dwelled with the numbers, trying to bring them together to form a uniform pattern for equations. They should have never stopped. They should have argued forever, questioned forever, and then... the two wizard-like giants would have found love and would have been brought back to earth. Uniformly, they would have been caught smiling by a photographer. And bombs would have not been needed from their equations.

The Universe Has Infinite Parts
Ready For A Unified Theory

'*M*ath comes back to one. We give it time.' Jim's teachers said that every day of his life in public schools in this small part of the dirty megalopolis that is Cleveland. Similar things in different ways happened to Jane. From the outside, one would feel there was a huge amount of quietness in their worlds. Inside, the world's constant motion was occurring. Time and movement were absolutes in their dizzying lives. Work and sleep took up the bulk of the time and movement. Things were going to change. Yet, the specifics were not known.

Both, at different times in their lives, saw that light was neither inside, nor outside of their worlds. Not yet. The selves were seeing the pulse of this visitor within. As the light gained strength, both saw that the world had turned around as they matured. Their attainments consisted of light. Both went to church. Both had pastors that understood patience. Yes, they had heard the same quote from each pastor that patience was a virtue. Both were preached to that heaven is open and the earth is broad and that things will occur as they were meant to occur. As they came into middle-age, they both felt love was proceeding at love's pace, and that was fine. Sure, if thoughts came, they investigated them. They did not sit around the house all day and wait for love to come. If tiny information came into their heads and the data sparked something within, they went after the knowledge with full force. Neither made an issue that, at many times, nothing substantial happened. Both never questioned God. Bother never questioned events. They had obtained flexibility in their middle years.

Sure, the turning around of the day is sometimes stopping all the progress. Jim and Jane did not think much of it. They smiled, went to sleep, and got up the next morning to face the day. Their light was seeing. Their light was inside, happy to breathe its own slow fire-life. They pushed into the future, not truly knowing when goodness would appear.

One day, Jane's thoughts came rapidly, and she did not fret. She jumped thoroughly into the rapid speed and did her best. Everyone liked her attitude about such things. Jane thought that thoughts were as quick and countless as breaths. And she was happy to know this. Never dallying, she looked forward to the dead days as much as she looked forward to the lively days.

Jane knew it was impossible not to have thoughts. Even at rest, she dreamed fantastic intricacies, and sometimes they came true. One night she dreamed that her car would fail, but that a neighbor would come over that next morning and notice that the battery terminals were corroded, and just needed to be brushed clean and that it would start. And it did, and, of course, she thanked Mrs. Roderick and gave her a hug, which made the older lady's day.

Jim noticed that the spirits within gave him a clarity that both heard and saw everything. It was all put together in an instant if Jim allowed the connections. He saw a fire on the way to work. He stopped the car. He gave himself a second or two before he got out of the vehicle. In his mind, he saw an animal inside the vacant house. He ran over and cracked open the back door. Two cats fled. The fire engines came; a fireman asked him if everything was okay. Jim said, "Yes, I am fine and so is our world." The hook and ladder doused the flames in minutes.

Their minds moved the energy the two lovers had within. These stable souls felt unified and stable and one, and they had not met. Or had they? The details did not flow. But, need details always flow? The big picture for this man and this woman was wildly apparent and gave them the peace they desired. God was on their sides, in their hearts, around their psyches, and within their ideas of time.

Stillness/quietude.

In general, the contractions of these two references, these two dear people accompany the expansions of awareness, and the expansions accompany the contractions of the truth within their love. If what was going to be done through awareness is done by all the rules of love, then the form of love must grow; multiply like it is not math and should not be math, but an entity of delight that is always unsolvable. Rules need not be rules. But they are, fine; the rules of love and lovers.

Just like the expansions in love, of which all are images, the expansion of time happens, originally, of its own accord. Love at first must seem like a strange procedure, and therefore, many call rules into it, permitting it. Both saw as they considered love, that they must forget the rules and proceed with abandonment. The accord within love saves the convention of its attention. Let any form of love be multipliable or divisible without limit. Infinity and love are the same if two are willing to allow the flow of the emotion. Jane and Jim were examples of this tiny particle. And their vision of the expansion of the emotion would be so massive it would not be seen. Like space. Space is so vibrant that it is never seen.

The primitive equations within love are never known. Yet, they are infinitely old and delicate and as precious as the God which rides over us. Primary math is more serene than the recent advanced math, even though solutions are rarely accurate. Such is love. Yes, the new, advanced and insane math is frivolous. Love is the basics. One plus one does equal two. And the two are one in an infinite space. The two are massive in weight. Massive in importance.

Again, CNN is here, in El Paso, on the border of Texas and Mexico, with a late-breaking story. A man has hijacked an eighteen-wheeler here and is driving it recklessly around the outskirts of this fine city in the American Southwest. We news folks are afraid of the death this man may bring to this quiet city in Texas. However, things have been quiet. The latest happening has to do with mailboxes in a development. Let's see the replay. Please run this, Jerry. See, right now, the huge, one-hundred-ton vehicle running into mailboxes on the side of the road. Wow, bam, it is devasting, and we are sure the U.S. mail will issue some charges against this hijacker. Check out the replay again. It is ultimate terror. It is bad to get caught... Now, back to your regularly scheduled news show from Atlanta... There are some breaking stories we are told happening at this very moment... We will be back with more news from the chaotic law-breaking of a supposed drunken truck driver in El Paso, Texas...

Lake Erie's blue within the lowest part of the sky is as deep as its name. The hue makes Jim want to spend hours looking at the horizon on perfect, cloudless winter days. It seems to him that he can see the peace that perfect love infects within you. Love was on the other side of the horizon this day. But it was coming. Jim could feel it like he could feel the sun rise in the morning.

Jim still thought about his oldest brother, the one that realistically was not with him. Still, this older man brought Jim the peace he was experiencing about time. Time was all around and never around, once one brought the burden of existence to its knees. Jim had done this. So had Jane.

After work that night, Jim was taking a walk in the Buckeye neighborhood. Four doors down, the Gibbons family had a cherry tree in their double lot. The wild cherry tree sometimes spoke to Jim on his walks. The nexus with the sky spoke with the twin-forked trunk of the tree. The bark smelled of cough drops. The nameless blue sky of that winter night allowed the tree to press upwards eighty feet, casting the shadows of its two umbrella-like trunks over the bedroom in his house. Jim wished to possess the spirit of the rum cherry. The trees' oblong crowns bared the queues of their future spring's white flowers. The flowers would become sewn into thin braids coming in the next season.

Could this mean that the hot, vicious storms of May would not jounce the monstrous limbs of this tree? And drop them on the house of this rich man, this man who could afford a house with two lots? But this family had children. Jim prayed nothing would occur. That it would only happen in his mind and be his misery, not another's truth.

Yet, Jim felt that the spirit in the tree did not support families. Part of his nightmare world thought that the cherry would fall when the chaos that is with nature calls upon its own drunkenness and appears and hurts others. Jim wondered whether prayer would have an effect on nature. Still, this man prayed. He always prayed when he knew nothing he could do would help. Of course, he prayed often.

Jim asked forgiveness for brewing up this mess. He thought he would rather experience hell than hurt the children of this family. He wanted his neighborhood to be fine.

Jim said, "In my closing is my beginning. Father, I am not worried about these neighbors. I will not bother you anymore with my foolishness. You have freshened me with your wild cherry tree. I hope that only my evil created this dismal story. I hope, and I pray."

God's honesty thrust his name into his heart. Jim thought that love was approaching just like the limbs of a tree. He knew the branches would fall delicately, not hurting, but bringing the assurance that many times things happen, and no one is hurt, and even are blessed, because they have been missed by terror. These stories did not get in the paper. It was funny how people talked about these stories all the time. Yet, they never made the news. Only dismal things make the news. But in everyone, many good things happen, happen, happen.

Time Can Be Measured More Accurately Than Inches

*J*ane and the days passed in Jim's head. "What will she truly be like, my love, when I am with her in the flesh?" Jim remembered the argument they had had weeks before. The argument was healthy and had made him wish to understand her even more. "That was love," he thought. "I love her. And I believe she loves me. Yes, we can argue and still love, still love, still deeply love each other."

Yes, the lady and Jim were the same age, lived within the same vicinity (the Buckeye section of Cleveland, which was once a highly ethnic section of the town but was now multi-racial and suffering from a lack of jobs and places to shop), and both worked downtown. Different from Jim, Jane liked her job as the head of an industrial real estate firm which was in Terminal Tower, the second highest building in the city. The saving of money and the improving of each business' promotional outline appealed to the artistic side of the lady.

And Jane knew that if she put herself out in the world love would find her. Aggressive in life and passive with love were her foundations. She thought that was the way it was supposed to be in life for women in America.

Jane was a pretty girl when she was young. The innocence of youth put a smile on her face. At the age of eight, she was five feet tall and did not get much taller as the years added themselves to her calendar. The one she kept throughout her life. The one she had the word love written on for each month of the year. The one that had all her appointments inscribed for each day to keep her organized, and they were printed and highly legible. The young lady had dishwater blond hair, thin ankles, a pert nose, and a lovely smile that almost always preceded each word that came from her mouth. Jane's parents treated their only child in a liberal fashion, allowing her to join the clubs and activities she was attracted to, and giving her all the positive feedback that they could give as she became a young woman. She attained good grades, graduated, and went on to get her Master's in Business Administration from Cleveland State University in the spring of 1974.

There were a couple of close calls as far as affections in college, and two after she graduated, but nothing serious. Love seemed to be on the lady's outskirts. Caring was around, kindness flirted with her, but love never beamed its eyes into her aura. Time was right with her. She always felt everything was fine. Time felt good in the lady's eyes. Jane appreciated it, loved it, and as a good lover, let it be. She cared about it more than the few half inches that were adding to her waist as time passed. She walked and kept herself in good shape.

This day, Jane wore a baby blue chiffon dress to work. She was trying to get rid of winter. She knew the spring color would brighten her day. "Good morning, this is Jane, may I help you?" Jane answered each phone call that she had on the job like it was someone she should know and care about, someone she wished to talk to about anything they wanted to discuss. When her underlings answered, they conducted themselves the same way because they were around her. You didn't know it, but she had this kind of effect on everyone within a few feet of her. Jane did not have to tell them how to conduct their business. The woman led by example. She did things right. With a smile on her face and a melody within her heart.

"Yes, I have the time for you. When can you come in? I would enjoy talking to you."

"Good, after your workday is completed. I will pick you up at Hopkins. No problem."

"I would be delighted to meet with you in our offices here in Terminal Tower. It has a sad name but is a fine, old building here in town. We will discuss your options."

"Yes, there is plenty of prime business real estate within the city. And fair prices are always available."

"You need not worry about daytime security here within the downtown area. But you will need to hire a security person for the night hours. I want to always be honest with you. It's a growing town now, and with that, problems arise."

"Yes, I will always be honest with you. Thank you. I always wish to help you. I know from experience that starting a new business can be difficult."

"For your business, I envision that you will need at least an entire floor of one of our larger buildings. I will have information accumulated about inexpensive phone services, snow removal, and utilities. My heart is on your side."

"I will also have info about athletic clubs, restaurants you and your employees might use, and parking, which we have a lot of within the city at reasonable rates compared to other metropolitan areas in the Midwest. I will be with you 24 hours a day, guiding you through all these possible hindrances."

"Please give me your e-mail address and fax numbers. I will treat them with the highest security. You can trust me. My reputation has no flaws."

"Might there be a time when I can speak to those above you if they wish more information? All bosses have important concerns that must be satisfied."

"So, are we standing on solid ground as far as we have gone so far? Are there any hesitancies?"

"Good."

"Very good."

"Super!"

Efficient and pleasing, the keys to Jane's life in the big world of American capitalism made her a lady on the way up in her complex world. Days went by, things went well, and Jane's salary and bonus compensation increased. Ah, life was fine, but where was love? Sure, Doubting-Thomas-kind-of-thoughts entered Jane's mind. But not for long.

Jane never panicked. Time did not disturb the woman. Love came when it came. Love was a different world from business. A gift that had no calendar. A gift. Yes, the lady always had strong thoughts within her mind.

The Light That Left Jane's Friend, Left Years Ago

*T*his is my testimony, a time in high school that rattles within my desperate heart. I am Julie. I am five-two, Black, beautiful, intelligent, and proud of all those characteristics. I am tough, but sometimes not so proud of that quality.

The day was about over, at least, for me. I wanted to catch the midtown bus, be home and in bed in an hour, watch some bad Saturday TV and be zonked out in fifteen minutes. The timer would click the tube off at eleven. Then all would seem fine and in line with my life.

Yes, so tired; but first I would use the toilet in the department store, Higbee's, and catch the transit bus home. With my plastic bags full of Christmas gifts, I would step into the women's lavatory and do my personal work and perform a rite to end this boring, seemingly relentless American custom to spend money for the holidays, and then filter out into the cold streets of Cleveland to find the bus stop and catch a noisy ride home to my apartment ten blocks east in Buckeye.

A clerk helped me, pointed, whispered over there behind hosiery. I slowly walked to the always dirty destination. I opened the self-closing door, entered and set the bags down. No one else was using the room, although it looked like it hadn't been cleaned in months. Single tissues of toilet paper dotted the floor. A small puddle near the ornate sink made the floor slippery. A few names on the walls bored me because no nasty comments were attached to them. I gingerly approached the toilet; one of those big, old ones with the lovely chrome handle and all white porcelain bowl, closed the door and began to unzip my slacks. Then I spotted the name painted with fingernail polish on the side of the dirty toilet - J. Jones, 1974. My mind shifted into another mode, one in which it seemed my whole life took a slant that would never bring it back to the normalcy it experienced day to day in this mid-sized mid-American city. I felt I was entering a world of daydreams; beautiful episodes of the way life should be in a normal world.

I coughed when I unzipped my department store slacks and began to let my waters run; just one cough in which, afterwards, my urine quickly flowed. The room with all its ornate fixtures resonated the sounds of the bubbly yellow wash, my middle-aged life running away. My mind got used to it, like it did every year my father took mom and me to Niagara Falls to see the Canadian side of the attraction. I laughed out loud when I began to think of Jim Jones and what I envisioned the first time we met at Collinwood H.S. in Cleveland. I had just moved in from Kamloops, B.C., and was a bit nervous. Pretty, delicate, and polite, my new girlfriend, Jane Smith, introduced him to me.

Jim said, "Good to know you," and I said, "You don't know me yet, but you will." He laughed quietly with his right hand gently covering his soft lips. Jim never found out that I loved him immediately. Jim left and went to class. I stared at him and smiled like I had seen a dream and realized it was real. He laughed again and apologized, and I said, "For what?" Jim said, "I said the wrong thing." I said, "You could never say the wrong thing," which reddened his cheeks, and he retreated back into the crowd and found his way to class. I think I remember the class was Algebra I with fumbling Mr. Rowly. Later that day, I waited around and watched him board his bus for his ride home. I stepped up to my bus and spent the slow time on the way home thinking about calling him and what I would say over the phone. It was a dream. I knew that we girls did not do that kind of thing, then or now.

Jim had stepped into my life, and I discovered I needed him and the feelings he gave to me. I also realized that I was not good at knowing whether the one I loved loved me. It didn't seem to matter to me. Or maybe I thought it was wrong to know too much about such things. It was hard for me to know what the other one felt about me deep in his heart. I stepped into love and found out it was more complex for me to understand than any word problem in Algebra I.

I took the chance and called Jim that night. I got his number from Jane, and at the spur of the moment, I just buzzed him and started talking. I don't even remember what I said. I talked fast, rattled on about school and sports and the like, and barely gave him a chance to talk about his life. He was kind and let me spew on. At the end of our conversation he said he looked forward to seeing me the next day. After I hung up, I took time to evaluate the conversation and felt like it had not gone well and that I would probably never get him to smile at me again or ever go out with me. Happily, I was wrong. Jim smiled at me the next day before his Algebra class, and he asked me to go out the next weekend. We went to the local Big Boy for a burger and fries, and then we parked somewhere. I did not attempt to kiss him because I did not want to scare him. I went home with him and told him I had had a nice time and walked with him to my door. Love was beginning to blossom, and all was well.

Weeks passed. Jim and I were working out fine. I walked with him to class. We dated every weekend. We kissed, soft and long kisses that tasted like love. I got to know his parents and we laughed over my dumb jokes and the sweetness of the pages of homework we would complete as our time together lengthened. My parents also got to know Jim, and my dad even told me one night he thought he was something special. We walked hand in hand to every class on his schedule. All the teachers looked at us and smiled. Yes, all was going well. Then, the bottom dropped out.

News came down the line that Jim's family was having problems; nothing specific. His father, something about him. Jim called to tell me. I just stuttered an okay and that we would keep in touch and hung up the phone. I took a walk and cried and asked God for reasons. The only answer I received was the quiet of the early winter when all the leaves are off the trees. The whole episode became a blur. I faked my way through classes and faked my way with Jim and our last days together as a couple. I never cried in front of him. I kept my bravery and made life keep going. Love never came to me again.

I went on to college and never met anyone of any worth there. I gave up on Jim after some letters that I had sent to him never were answered. Time rushed on, and I never felt the way I felt with Jim again with other men in my desperately disappearing life. Got a degree, worked, and earned enough money to have a nice car and a big TV set, and that was just enough to keep me going. Then this event, the lavatory, and his name and the date. All the massive memories came swirling back. I started thinking about why the name was there. I mean, was it the same guy, or someone entirely different, and what did all this have to do with the date next to it—1974? What did it all mean?

I talked to no one. My parents had both passed on years before, two years apart. Friends at work became just that. I never socialized with them outside of the job. Shopping for decent clothes became a pastime I did not enjoy anymore. Reading the newspaper became a way to waste time. Going to the library and taking out old novels became a hobby. Jim and his ruggedness had fallen away from me. Now he was back, and I thought maybe he was back to stay. I made no effort to contact him. His memory became enough for me. His beauty tripled. His voice softened and sounded alluring. His personality became beyond any words I could imagine. I felt like my mind had married him. My soul desperately fell into his arms. I came back to the bathroom often, did my business, and left with a loving joy; a quiet way to live a life unfulfilled. Middle age made me understand that the sweetness in life, the true wonder, are the memories of the way things were when times were simple and direct and protected from the complexities of other people's dismal worlds. The purest form of love was the memory of a man who was perfect. His life was controlled by forces beyond the yearnings of a young woman growing up in a mid-American dream. I never had a thought again about why his name was written in a lavatory. I never questioned again whether it was his or not. I went to see J. Jones, 1974, occasionally, to wake up my imaginary world and let it reside with the chaotic yet boring stillness inside of me. A world I chose to live. One in which love is only within the heart.

"God Abhors A Naked Singularity." Roger Penrose

*J*ulie casts a shadow. That's what friends do at times. Still, Jane sees that love is coming. She knows that love is her future. Jane knows that love is beyond the word beautiful. The light, the shadow, and the contrasts. All form love in varied ways. Jane's singularity was moments in days. The future still lived within her. Time was the arrow that directed her to be patient with ever-present life.

Cobalt blue defined Jane's eyes. The blue waited to be shown in a deep way, on a sunny day in spring, after lonely winters leave, and as the sky's deep horizon wore a type of beauty with the day. Yes, Jane's lover would see the blue as the most pleasant color he ever saw. Ever.

Jane would arise. No one was in her house, the one she bought with hard-earned money in Buckeye, the one that was a two-story colonial she bought with the intention of making spotless and perfect, a lovely nest. Jane always arose early, showered, worked with her plants (the Dieffenbachias, the firs, the mums, and the funny little trees that live, yes, live in her bungalow), dusted her fine furniture, took her dirty clothes to the basement, and sat down to plan her endless day. At times she allowed the quiet to be interrupted by a Mozart sonata from Horowitz, or if she was in a mathematical mood, a Bach sonata, a violin played with no emotion from Gidon Kremer. This slight lady would sit at her refinished desk and do a little paperwork, the bills or a letter to her mother.

A flow would enter her, especially when the Bach would play, like it was being played without an effort. She would continue to go backwards in time. Let her mind flee into an endless peace. She knew the flow worked for ancient Egyptians who surveyed their land, using triangles to give equal shares of plots hear the Nile to its citizens. Pythagoras and his symbols for the large group, all the diagonals flowing in his mind throughout the landscape and how these triangles would bring peace to the countryside. The days, the plots, the time, and the way things in the minds of quiet folks make an endless dream for them in the simple things they do in day-to-day remotely intelligent life.

And when Christ came. The forms conceived by him of finite cardinal numbers that made unlimited crosses in the countryside. How he expressed the lines without speaking. All those simple expressions in the endless crosses, the steps to a calculus that has not been conceived yet but will be. All are integrals and numbers and will be constructed if we allow time to pass and not be so inclined to work for the solutions. The proofs are in space. The proofs exist in their own infinities. Deepest space. Oh, to have all problems have solutions within the moment the problems arise. Call that space, heaven, and know it is coming. Jane thought, "But wait...please wait...do your dishes...dust your bookcase...

work...go home...and wait. All will be well. Wait. Yes, all love will live within my heart. I will wait. Wait and smile."

The lines were within the space. There were all the crossed lines. The cross, and the simple walking, and the standing, and all the talking to friends and non-friends. Time never crawled into the supposed chaos, even though it is not, and crawling out and being visible when it needs to be visible, and all the repetition. Jane felt each moment and knew the love of loves was coming. Each repetition resulted in a new arrangement, like ones before, but different in many ways. One cross meets another. One is formed this time, a perfect one, with Jesus attached and smiling. Still, it is in its own cross and alive and it works and when the time comes, a child comes. And all the work seems to be done, a peace is felt, and the peace is synonymous with love. The love lives on and is handed over at a certain time to the child. We are always taught we are all children, all children when we consider the vastness of what can be known.

Jane thought that all repetitions are finite. They lead to the love. The cardinal number is one. One is from two. One and one is... Two can become one. "Wait...wait...I will wait." Jane saw all that was life in Buckeye, prepared herself for work, worked efficiently, and waited in her beautiful house on Woodhill Road off Buckeye for time to pass, left most of the control to a God who resides in an old part of Cleveland.

An empty cross now.

All would eventually be vindicated in a space that has a marked state of love. The canon, Jane's law, was an agreement, not a dominance.

A conversation appeared between the two lovers, "The life of our love's spirit comes from the prior death of our minds." Jane felt the words coming from an unknown source and celebrated that fact when she added, "I am happy this is coming out, and I do not know where it is deriving itself. But I feel our minds are being killed because love feels it wishes to replace them. The concentration. The quietism is divided among us. Yet it is bringing us into a wonderful whole."

Jim worked up courage and spoke, "Violins have been screeching at me. And I have listened. But, yes, I have been waiting also. Now I feel. I feel we are in an adagio. My distractions meant my mind was racing. I did not wish for oblivion because I meant my spirit to be clear. I wished it to be clear so that it could accept love because love was arriving. Love was near, so near."

"I love you. I wish my words were truth. But I will wait for them to catch onto time. When I have seen you in dreams sitting, I knew you were unifying your energy and waiting." Jane lowered her head and gazed at the soil. At this time, it was good to be outside of her residence, being with her small garden and her tended lawn. "Do not let my ears hear what you are saying, but rather what you are feeling as you gaze at me. When you do not hear my breathing, my breathing is fine and in line with what will eventually occur. My mind is cleared for you. Yet, my heart is full, full of the love it has for you. Yes, it will always be full of your tenderness."

74

Noise was coming. Way off. Yet, it was all around in this age. Noise would always be. The sad perplexity of it all. But we are not to question it. No. Never. Just bust through it and be alive. With love.

This is CNN... The chase continues... the noise is deafening and real, yet it is not totally disturbing this western, spanish town of El Paso, that is the outskirts... cops continue to chase an eighteen-wheeler, one we have finally found out who owns, consolidate freight, out of midland, Texas, the driver has talked to the police and offered his view of what happened... we have that report... "I was getting my bill of laden in the terminal... Came outside to begin my trip to deliver a load of boxes to an undisclosed industry in Chicago... and lo and behold, my truck was taken... I mean, that is the extent of my story"... Wow, can you believe this driver's simple tale?... we will continue as the day progresses.... and the hum of this adventure brings in more facts... no accidents yet.... but, is this an accident waiting to happen?...

The dreams continued. At night, during the day. Time did not matter because the deep dreams cast their glow.

"When you sink into oblivion, time stills, but is a life over? My friend, why did she choose to end her life as she lived?" Jane stuttered, almost cried when she relived this story.

"I love you."

"I... I know." Jane knew the healing and lived on. "I will get up and take a walk. Sure, it is best to sit when sitting is called for, but the early morning will liven me. I will feel free when I see the morning awake."

"I love you."

"I know, I know. No need to keep repeating." She knew this was stupid of her. Jane thought but did not say, "There are many falls in front of a steep cliff. The trees by its edge wither with the death. I should stay away from such places now that I have love." She bowed her head to cry for a last time. Yet, she did not know this was the last time she would cry, the very last time. She quit tearing as her head rose, her face smiled into the light that was the new day.

"I, I love you."

"I do not have much on my mind." Jim looked over to his life and smiled at it. He waved at it. A goodbye to the old, old, deadened times. A last goodbye. "I can be free. I can now live. I will make my mood gentle for you and wait for you to move, then I will move with you. The music will play if we wish it to play. You will let me choose the music. Our minds will be comfortable. And we will enter an eternity with a love that is bound by ribbons that last."

"It is nice now to sit inside of love, and not the void that we had accepted for so long." Jane, in her fifties. Jim, in his fifties. Time, never a number. Jim now let thoughts enter and be said if they wished to be said. "The shadow world is gone. The deadness, the dumb meditations, the hollow means of going from place to place with ugly music playing loudly and distracting your fortitude."

Jane whispered, "Yes, if we would have continued this way for long, we would have shriveled."

"The myriad, slender pipes of love called. The bright moon is in mid-sky as the sun rises and brings its warmth. The entire earth, which I now see fully, is a realm of light." All were ghostly days of the past. Jane saw a face that brought a gift. It was not a pretty face. But it was a face she knew somehow. Jim's raw face burned for her. That is all she knew. That was all she needed to know.

"Higher." Jim screamed into the moon. "Higher good is what I know now. The water is pure. Our shame is gone. The flawless love of God had come to their haunts, as one, and they were seeing time ripen, and they knew now they would come together at some point as all stories continue, as all glee continues in realms that have no words to truly describe it.

Jane went to a deaf man's house. She did not know the man's name, another of those she met that she knew was not her love. To enter his house, she needed to feel dead on earth. He had a vision though and she was interested in it. He was an aesthetic, and he sat a lot at his desk or on the rug in his living room or, on rare occasions, out within his tiny lawn even in winter. It was sad. He always hoped for the best. But the best never came.

One day, Jane talked with him. I mean, yes, you can talk with him, but it is rare. He did not respond to this day very well. He was beginning to smell bad. His caretaker must have taken a vacation while on the job. The Buckeye section of this part of the city did not know anything about this man. Jane got up the courage and visited with him. The smell was him. She viewed his newest poem, one he had written on a pad because the computer in his home had died of old age. The ode was whole. It said, "Elezan tur Zo. Buur rafer me, me ote seed. Yoursef me to oter to red thus, and me rede and me lov and me..." Jane loved the poem and it stayed within her mind, one she would recite to herself when she got married in one of Christ's churches in this old part of town. The man made her smile. Even though many times he would be odorous. This time his smell meant death to him. A death with an aroma around it so no one need come see it and be with it.

The health of this part of town was indifferent. The innocence of nature was reliable. The beneficence of this area and its trees, its flowers and its way to clean itself up after a hard snow was all about the way the city was in America. Such was the health and the cheer and how they afforded a forever in two minds who took walks, and now would finally meet. No reasons to grieve at this time. Nature was controlling the flower. It was not grim at all. To look out and see good things each day, then work and come home and breathe in the magnificent gift of love. Jim and Jane and Buckeye. Coming together in a common unity. The positive sides of regular life decided they could see them and be with them. The two pretended they were simple minded. In truth they were. They were getting a rest from their fellow man by finding love and a few words.

Gravity Is A Consequence Of The Fact That Space/Time Is Not Flat

*J*im was thinking about his brother, the one that died at birth, the one that would have been older than him. The story's desperation was seeking Jim's core. Sure, things were going well. It looked like love was coming into his life for real. Yet, doubt was creeping into his mind's vocabulary. Maybe the man was thinking too much. At that time, America was too much. The TV. Cars. Jobs.

A deep snowstorm was adding its gray coldness to the February winter sky. Inches were adding up quickly on the city's streets. The lake effect was coming straight from the north, and Buckeye had the weather's hum in its air. Maybe this, maybe the fact that time was getting to Jim made the future of love seem far away. Jane was drifting in and out of his memories, good memories. Yet, the corroded ones were bearing rust and roughening up Jim's hopes.

This late winter's day was taking the color blue from his eyes. Gray seemed to pervade his mood, the colors of love in his heart, and the dullness of the future of a long winter.

Jim was weathering a rehearsal for silence. In his daydreams, the woods were becoming unnamed. The green that usually is the woods in spring sparkled through all the unnamed plants. Jim never understood why scientists put names to all of them. He thought nature wanted us to leave them alone. Jim always thought that they hurt the plants as much as those who cut them down and put poison on them. Evil was evil to this man. The sun knew the plants did not have labels on them. If the sun did not shine for the botany of the woods, the plants would go away quietly, like a suitor who cannot make eye contact with a lovely woman, and then, the plants would sprout elsewhere in a place where they were welcome.

The ground was soft and although his bare feet got soiled, Jim did not mind. Jim noticed his feet were not cold, and that he could hear the music through the trees. The music of a front. Quiet was most of life. But then, fronts would come to northeast Ohio, and the noise of nature would surround the day. Jim was happiest when noise was around.

Over and over, in his dreams of summer, Jim looked around, even though he felt like an odd tourist. He did not care that he was staring into the wonder that was the woods. Love continued to be in the air. The greenness in the plants, the lush life of their oxygen, and the interest in the moments presented themselves to his weathered eyes, eyes that had not seen much in a long life.

In this daydream, Jim saw a fire in the distance. He was feeling like his mind was taking him to Patagonia to be with the natives and to experience nature as they entangled its maize and grew a peace about life and death and the wind. The fire looked alone.

It flickered and warmed a small area. Jim did not know how it was started. The mysticism of the moment made his heart brew for desire. Jim was getting to a point where he wanted to touch everything. He was growing tired of dreaming of everything. No one was around. Jim was not even wondering how the fire was started now. Jim was not feeling fear this moment. The wind was shifting, still strong, but it was heading in an opposite direction. It was not important, specifically in what direction.

A lovely sunlight through all the verdant trees was painting halos of yellow on the soft ground around this paradise. Jim was feeling a magic in this trip. He felt like he was seeing photographs, but they were not important. Jim was feeling what his life was, and that was not important. The future seemed to be accessible, and it was going to be a good journey, no matter how many down days were included within it. The future was fine.

Time seemed as slow as a massive body on a slow earth.

The weight of the future was a fine thing to carry. All within Jim's life seemed to be headlines that never made the papers.

Jim felt like his hermitage was being emptied, and he had no complaints. Sure, he felt a little down. Those on the street who giggled when they saw the man did not matter anymore. The weight was taken from them. Love was better than any laughs.

This quiet one saw that the emotions of love came from the single node of a fir tree, one that grew in another land, far away. It came as time allowed to his home, his heart. To Jim, it felt like it was a rainy place, one that was always warm and fruitful.

Love was expanding on the globe. The chaos of continual war. Famine. Politicians and their many words. None of this felt very important. Jim had read, and he felt there were purposes, even to his reading, that scientists were reporting that the sun at one time was upside down. Supposedly, this event occurred when the dinosaurs roamed the earth. Jim was starting to see significances to everything. Love was making him see more clearly.

Jim read that his religion, Christianity, had a gnosis within it. This symbol consisted of a cross with a super globule embedded in the middle, the intersection of the two lines. Jim, at first, cried when he read this. Later, he smiled as God shone down on him how the men of science and religion were stupid and full of their own egos. God was telling Jim not to deeply listen to any men of learning. He was being told to listen himself to his own depths.

At work, one of Jim's secretaries said that men who study humor were finding out that the tickle that had inspired laughter was getting lost from newborn babies. That this continued laughter would be lost forever. Like it was evolving and dying out. Jim laughed at his secretary. The young lady cried in the lavatory after this meeting. Jim did not hear her tears. He was too busy listening to his own emotions. And to Jane's.

In his old car, Jim heard a bang. Thought it was his car hitting a deposited tire laying in the road, but found out that it was the theory coming into his head. The big bang was just another male scientist's way to explain God's orgasms. That mass destruction was just another tragedy thought up by an ardent science writer. That bangs were mostly man-made. And Jim knew he meant the word man in a literal sense.

Jim wanted to think dirty. He had a supposition. He felt the word fuck was used too often on the east coast, not at all on the west coast, and the right amount in the Midwest. Still, he thought the whole country had problems with dirty words. They seemed to be dull reactions to dull subjects or crises.

A blacklegged Kittiwake sat on Lake Erie's water in its winter plumage and spoke to Jim every few moments. Jim felt like the bird was screaming at him. Telling him to wait. That love would come, that he should not be a complainer. The ugly bird was telling Jim not to enter his territory. That the bird owned that land, that the bird was the main moaner in this area of the country, and that that was fine, and okayed by a bigger God. The bird was telling Jim to consider himself small. Like he was any kind of bird. And all of this did not matter. Jim listened. Jim was thinking. His mind, his soul, his depths were all taking in what they were supposed to take in. Everything.

A lone meadowlark dove at the bird in the water. Still. He never landed. The noise was becoming the chaos in a bad, new age piano composition. Jim did not notice the meadowlark. His mind did not register if he saw something enharmonic. The meadowlark was an eastern bird and a western bird. The bird was not supposed to be flying around Midwestern winter skies. Jim had shut his mind to chaos at this moment. Certain things were not supposed to happen. Certain other things were happening. Jim was aware of them.

Math was forming circles in the moment. Jim thought, "The simplification of the symbol of love is unique. If an expression of love simplifies to a simple expression, then this expression cannot simplify to an expression other than love. In simplifying love, we may have many choices in the steps. Thus, the act cannot be a unique determinant of love unless we can find in it a form independent of all the choices." Jim was at work during this moment, this moment that lasted a millionth of a second. He did not answer any phones during this moment. He was concentrating on every aspect of deep kindness.

Now, it was clear to Jim that for some expressions of love, the hypothesis does provide a unique determinant of the big value, and then the phone rang and Jim got off his math. Zero came into his life. The unmarked state entered him. The death of a unity theorem zeroed into him. The slaying of axioms zapped at him. The dismissal of mass collided inside of him. The dominance of the true meaning of love came liltingly into him and resided, and he knew it was awesomely near. That love had no way to be discovered unless God discovered it for you and gave it to you unlocked. The whole stock and barrel beautified his realm.

Joe Taylor, El Paso, and the truck, the colossal truck keeps plowing along on the interstate down here. We have a name now. The man who hijacked this mother-sized rig is John Smith. Yes, this is correct and has been confirmed. The tough story continues. And we will be here to give it to you as it happens. A copter got down close enough a few minutes ago to see that Mr. Smith had a smile on his weathered face. Yes, the man is old. And balding and wearing fatigues. More on this breaking story later. Now back to the headline news at CNN... we will keep you posted...

Jim was hearing echoes in the Cuyahoga River Valley. And he was okay with the noise. He was sitting, and the spirits were entering him. The openness was extreme. Jim was hearing the people talking and was not caring about each word that was being spoken. Things were close but far away in the same instant. All things were not understood. This authenticating experience was bringing Jim closer to Jane. The light of Jim's eyes was blazing upwards. All the quiet was happening. Jim felt like he was opening his eyes with a cloud, and the moisture felt the quiet in his mind. Jim felt like an empty room containing light. His body felt like jade. He saw this room filling with love, and happiness, and kindness, and a thorough depth of true goodness. It was like he was coming into heaven.

Faith was coming after Jim on its own. The experience was pleasant. Jim was finding out that this practicing of turning the light around would have no effect on his normal job. All this was taking place before the job, during the job, and after the job. Jim felt a dialogue with God. God said, "When matters come up, one should respond, and when these things come up, one should discern them and act. Period."

Now, in the morning when this man woke to go to work, he awoke earlier. Sometimes at five a.m. Jim cleared all objects from his head. This was easy to do in the early morning when the sun had not begun to rise. Jim quietly laid in bed and let his mind drift to where it was supposed to go. It was then that he felt free. Jim's essence was to act purposefully without striving for any one thing, except love. He felt centered and more alive than ever. Because Jim did not strive, he felt like he would not fall into the emptiness he had felt most of his life, like at times he was collapsed into a dead void. Jim's functions were centered. The mechanisms for his life were in his eyes. He felt the same about Jane. The four eyes were the handles of the stars. The cosmos at one time felt unapproachable to the two. Now, it felt like it was an adventure that was worth seeking. That, yes, one could venture among the starts and see beauty beyond the word beauty. Smiling as they fled old earth.

The creation of love was approaching. Yes, this sentence was said many times in his life. But now it did not feel so far off. But Jim knew closeness could not be measured.

Jim felt like water. Like he was a pond that held meaning. He lowered his eyelids and looked into the vast chamber of himself and saw the nothingness that he had seen before love came, and all this was worth its depth.

The ungraspable sense of space was evaporating. The chamber was filling with a product that was full of life's gifts and it was near. Jim felt the clouds filling a thousand mountains, and only he could see the vista and its every detail.

The living midnight was billowing away.

Time Is Slower Than A Large Body--Love Has Nothing To Do With Time

*T*he two had not met. Yet, Jane had lovingly become Jim's whole psyche. He didn't fell a load about this more called love. More and more, Jim felt like a nobody and an everyone at the same time. He used to care about himself in an odd, almost too antsy, way. Now, Jenny had grounded herself within Jim. He felt the love that had been vacant from him for thirty-five years since his mother's death from an accident when he was five. Jane was bound to him within her own spell upon this old earth. When she was not around in Jim's daydreams about her, he grew more and more to want to touch her delicate arms and gaze into her indigo eyes. When she finally did arrive, Jim embraced her gently and asked her if she was fine. Jane knew before this even happened that Jim meant this without any weight attached to the words. Each day, each moment. Her pleasures and needing were his. Nothing about her was logical or real. Jane knew life was a spurt and she was very willing to let it go and smile over its rushing moments. Jane had no ambitions that controlled her life like many women of the present do. It was like she took love-tranquilizers and laughed off the ego-mess of goal setting and getting ahead in America. Yes, it was all like some insane love song. She knew all about love and love's willingness to be unreal in a concrete world.

As a child Jim felt the beauty of his mother's breasts. His mother always seemed willing to let her love flow into him. He remembered every second with her and how father loved her as much as he did. All was the way it should have been, and then she was taken. Simple, wholesome life flowed away from him at that moment. Empty years passed. Jenny came to him in a breath. Jim's rich father had raised him well. He did well in the private elementary and high schools he attended. He received A's at Hirma College and went on to become the best he could be; attained his nice job and made decent wages.

A good case study. The boy had something tough happen in his life, overcame it by working hard, and became a successful man in business. No one had to worry about him. He was fine, but they did not know how empty he felt about this thing they easily call the good American life. They didn't notice that he did not smile often. Sure, he rarely frowned. But he was absent the big life.

Jane walked into Jim's sightscreen when she decided to work out during the winter at a spa instead of taking her usual walks around the neighborhood near their homes. Jim was pumping some iron, and his eyes caught Jane's beauty running the indoor track. Days went by and he kept seeing her. An intense feeling kept coming into the valves in his heart each moment she appeared. Like this was, he felt, the one. The one he had been having dreams about. At first, he couldn't figure it, then it hit him that he had found love. Or it had found him. She kept running; Jim kept watching. She kept pushing herself and Jim's love for her kept adding onto her mileage.

For years Jim had had an intense love in his mind for knowledge. His body felt the love of nature's earth, and that is why he got into being with nature and took long, arduous walks, but his heart felt nothing but the pumping of the organ. He lifted a few weights, and Jane entered the scene, and his nature changed. Jim felt her intense beauty, and his rational thinking turned to metaphor. Her sound was like the click of a perfect lid.

Things become chaos and had become chaos for Jim, but when he thought of Jane, when he heard his Jane, he was awakened to a peace beyond the words, and the noise and decibels of a dead life. She turned Jim quickly to thoughts of love, and that is what he needed. And after all his dreams of love and Jane, that is what he smilingly thought was his fate.

Jane has wholeness. The lady seemed complete and ready for the good and bad of wandering the planet within a pair. Jim looked to her to fill him when time grinds and twists edging on insanity and being a void. Jane had identity. She putts and grinds through her days with her beauty, and it did not affect her. She was not conceded nor convinced, just ready to meet each day with a smile. Jim had looked her up in the dictionary trying to find new words to describe her. She was a sensual passel of cells. Jane was like a willow in autumn. She drooped but still showed a green liveliness late in the season when all other trees have turned an ugly brown. And in spring she was the first tree to show fresh life in the form of flowing, soft leaves. Jim thought about her;

he had waited for her, and when she was ready, she would enter his life and bring a sweetness that he could feel like the minute tremor of the first drops of a spring rain. A slight hesitation that brings change to the fiber of the earth but does not hurt a man or anyone near. Jane shone within his life and continued to shine it up with each breath she took. Jim did not even consider why she didn't enter his life sooner. Jane and Jim were both middle-aged. Jim just thought about tomorrows when he could show her his love during the stilling days of new time.

In Buckeye, the birds came early this year. A Ground Dove sprang at the neighbors' window, looking at himself and seeing the love he was seeking in the clean windows. There were less crows than the year before. The robins had lasted the winter and looked healthier than ever. White Swans with their dirty behaviors stayed away from the few ponds that sat among the clean houses in the old neighborhood. Loons were heard flying overhead going to their homes in Ontario. Geese and their dirty feces stayed in other neighborhoods with dirty ponds. A few Sandwich Terns visited, like they were trying to see and understand what this human love thing was all about.

Jane's syntax was perfect. She moved together like words that are in phrases. Her beat was slow, but it never got out of whack. Her music was her diction. Jane talked to Jim with her silence, and he listened with every part of his frame. She was like an English class that works without error; one that is necessary because love is necessary; and Jim could hardly wait to grade her homework because he knew he would give her a fine grade because she was every good person in a perfect life. She was beyond mere words.

The flower was near, and it was real, and all things looked exciting to Jim. It seemed to the man that he had almost entered the world of utter quiescence where not a single new thought was ever born. Now, love was hitting him hard and tons of energy was seeking his moods. Jim, who had been gazing inwards was now not taking that journey, a fruitless one.

The center was approaching. Jim felt like neither destroying things nor contemplating things. Things felt wasted to him. Love centered him into a love of finding a good, decent life and staying with it. A love, a family, a smile. The white of the moon at night had become his sun. A warming vehicle that took nothing from him. Jim was willing to borrow this light and its warmness and pass it on to whomever he was with. "I know this is not mine, but I wish to give it to all." Ah, the love that was approaching was worth the wait for Jim. And he was feeling every morsel of it. No discrimination was needed between the light and the darkness in the Buckeye world. Elixirs had crystallized.

Water and fire. Both felt glorious. There was less silence, but the silence that came was fine. The changes of the world meant less and less. Jim used to worry about the milliseconds that could be seen. He used to study them. Now, he knew these were fruitless journeys. Heaven, great and small, the massive evil in a fixed world, chaos, the world politics on TV, the old, dying women on the street, how men died earlier than woman. The masses of unanswered questions now meant nothing to a man in love, in love with Jane.

Sure, Jane had her bad times, but the deprivation was minimal and always had a purpose. Jim gazed at her and saw that her steps flowed and allowed him to see a realm that was nescient and true to the purposes of real life. The energy of the conflict brought him to a phlegmatic peace, one that was solid in a jelling kind of way. Jane was sweet, even when her small flits into chaos came. This happy woman slept in the sun, and she repeated herself as she smiled in her dreams. And her words were always right. At times, Jim would hear her speak to someone near. And her voice sounded right.

Jim looked forward to, "Hey, I love you. What did you do today? I missed you. Let's sit down and talk about our days. I had a good day. Wasn't the day a nice one? My boss smiled at me. Everyone at work seemed to be doing okay. I don't understand your work, but I bet it is wonderful. How are your coworkers doing? Any happy things to say about their lives? Come on, come on, tell me, please." And Jim sputtered, but told her about the work. He explained to her everything about his job, but she still did not understand, and that was fine. Jim's dream world continued. He hugged her and told her he was glad she had such a good day. He hoped that was enough, and it was. Her words meant little to Jim. It was her sounds, the tones, her strong and lively sounds, that opened her love to him. And it lasted the whole next day. And she accepted him even when he was blunt and not ready to talk. Jane just busied herself doing something else.

Later on, they made love in a gentle way. Her soft love made grasps in her eyes when they opened and closed so delicately that

Jim could never tell when they were fully opened or closed. Her warming body, like in the spring, brought Jim leaves to soothe his brown and hardened trunk. Jim was barren until Jane entered him with her love. His breathing became metered because she was what she was. She was beyond any reason to figure. Jim was bound in her spell. Her pleasure increased and became his. He felt like a child and was consumed by her. Her breasts softened his will. Jim became hers. Jim went back to his childhood, but more than that, he leapt ahead to her fresh love and its future. Time stopped as if it had reached an undefined speed. All the glowing words stopped as Jim found that the feelings of love were non-syllabic and ghostly. All thoughts ceased. She had come within him. Jim said words beyond the sounds, and all things burst into godly thoughts. She was with him now. She was with him. That was all that was needed. She was with his complete self, in love, and he felt her love and reached for his. They would talk later more deeply when they had the time. Jane would go run after their lovemaking. Jim would watch her out the front window. She would be back before he knew it. Again, when she arrived, time would stand still.

At first, the thought of losing her brought shivers to Jim's simple brain. As the years would go by, he would think less and less about that journey of fear. More and more Jim would forget about the day they met at the gym or the specifics of their engagement, marriage, and their child. Jim just took as a gift her love, and that was enough, and he smiled openly about the gift.

Jim would die before their child would graduate from elementary school. Jane would cry. The child would cry, but not know why they were crying. For the first time in her life, Jane would feel down deep depression. For nearly a year, she would not understand why she did not care to do her usual things, feel her usual rhythms, and how she was beginning to feel a bit tired.

Then, different things would happen. Still, nothing was happening at this moment in both their lives. Yet, they felt all their lives were mapped out and were ready to occur. No one knew when.

"I love you" wanted to be spoken. The blues of the world were crystallizing into a cobalt blue that was indescribable.

All Galaxies Are
Moving Away From Us

*J*im, "I do worry about us." Jane quietly and quickly said
to him, "Me too." The dream continued.

Still, small doubts crop up in every dream. Jim and Jane felt
their love for each other falling away. Large, good things do bring
doubts to those who worry that dreams are only those whispers
that never multiply. Still, something inside the two told them that
this dream would see life, would multiply, and would last forever.

Outside events bring sarcasm into lives. Jim had been reading
snippets from kamikaze pilots. World War II was the man's fetish
along with other smaller desires. Jane would have to be ready to
accept these odd things in her man. His love of that war, his need
to buy plenty of CDs each month to satisfy his love of music, and
his eerie habit of growing beefsteak tomatoes in his small yard
each year in Buckeye.

"To My Honorable Brother, once again, there are orders
that have come down for the attack in which we will never return.
I feel not the slightest regret. Already I have grown intimate with
death, the ultimate character-building passage that we human
beings have to face. All that is left is to carry out the duties..." A

Lt. Yoshitaro scribbled a message to his brother and then went out to do his duty. Jim had a tear in his eye. At this moment he wanted to kiss Jane. She was not present. Jim read on. A Lt. Masahisa, at the age of twenty-five, wrote to his daughter in 1944, "Motoko, you often laughed when you looked at my face. You slept in my arms and we bathed together. Motoko, when you grow up and want to know about me, ask your mother. I left my photo at home for you. I thought of you becoming fine, gentle; a sensitive person. I named you Motoko." These were the tears in a life of one who was following a destiny that harmed the fabric of being a human. Jim read on, "P.S. The toy doll you had as a child I took with me in the airplane as a good luck charm--this way you are always with me. I tell you this because I think it would be wrong for you to know." Two men, Jim had read about in Manoa, a Journal published in Hawaii. The named given to this summer issue was Silence in Light. Jim thought in words to himself, "This silent foolishness. The ability to say no to anyone. This article defines, in a huge way, the essence of the American spirit. The essence is no. Our country celebrates the fact that we can say no to anyone at any time." Jim felt that 'yeses' for good things are what we are truly about. Jim had said plenty of yeses to Jane over the years that they had been together in dreams.

Jim wished to kiss Jane at this time. And he did.

He could see the event occurring. It would first happen in his home, under the photo he had framed of Honest Abe, the president who prayed desperately each day during his years in which he was trying to keep the country together, a marriage that seemed at the time to be moving towards a divorce. "Four score and seven years ago, our country brought forth on this continent a new nation conceived in liberty and dedicated to the proposition that all men are created equal." All concerning a battle that meant something, that was fought honorably. That was totally about liberty. Not about kamikaze pilots giving lives so that their nation could get larger. Freedoms were not included in their higher goals. They had no higher goals, except death. Love. A kiss. Both were included in Jane and Jim's higher goals. The kiss was coming. Many kisses were coming. Eternal love was here already and would continue. Love for the sake of love. An even, jubilant love. True to the bone.

Jane and Jim were at work when this event happened. Happened in two lives that were busy laboring. Dreams happen in instants. Jim was ready. Like most men, he initiated the action.

"And your day? Your day was fine?" Jane said, "Fine enough."

Jim, "You look lovely after your busy day at the office."

"And so do you."

"I wish... I wish..."

"It is okay to doubt.."

"I love you... I know I have said that to you..."

"I love you… I always wish to say that to you... Forever."

The event occurred and would occur for years afterwards, each day, into the infinity that is the thorough definition of time. A loving, romantic kiss. Not one to satisfy sexual needs, the moving lust that God has given all people, the ability to seize a life and control it and make your body feel a sensation that needs to be felt. Sure, that would be there for the two. But the eternal kiss was the one that they would use to define their lives. The kiss would be a clean symbol of God's gift to two.

This kiss was fine and alive and had no ulterior motives other than to express the deep, eternal love both had for each other. The kiss was wet. The kiss lasted only a moment. The kiss touched a God who felt it was his finest invention for two to express a momentous gift. The kiss lasted a moment but meant a touch that secured the desires in delicate fabrics that made touching them better than looking at them. Yes, the kiss came and stayed. The kiss stayed. The kiss, the first one, was in Jim's house and took place under his history. From then on, it would happen all over and be good all over, and would stay good all over, in his house, in her house, in their house, in the street, at work, during their marriage, during their honeymoon in the Bahamas, at relatives' houses, in malls, in church each Sunday, under the eaves of their new home, in their old car, in their new car, in bathrooms, even in the shower, among the lives and loves of many others at no specific times, then at some specific times, sometimes planned and at other times at the spur of a moment only God could define. A simple kiss whose complex thoughts made movements insignificant in a chaotic world. A world that was full of grief. This grief was always healed by a kiss.

"We should go shopping." The two start talking as one. "We should kiss and go shopping. We should kiss again. We should go shopping at Value City, where the poor are, and the prices are good, and we should kiss. We love to do this. This wrong side of town is the good side for life. We kind of like it. We should kiss. We will ask that woman over there with Jeans for her kids, and tops for her daughters and gym shoes for her boys what is the meaning of life. And she will say nothing at first, have a surprised look on her face. And we will kiss. And she will say 'You two sumthin.' and she will add one word, 'LUV.' And I will find a sports coat with one button missing and you will fix it and we will kiss. And you will find a spring dress with a dirty spot and I will take some cleaner that is good and dab the spot and it will be fresh again, and we will kiss. And I will tease you that one day I will be a better shopper than you and you will laugh that there are no cheap stores up in heaven because that is how long it will take for you to be a better shopper than you, and we will kiss. All the clothes are cheap but our kiss is free, and it will last longer than dresses or sport coats. We will then kiss." All things seemed to be better now. As Jim and Jane flow into a normal time that is life in a rich country, a country that has everything to experience, and that love is allowed and never injured by a big government.

The primary arithmetic of it all seeped into the scenes. Any crosses empty are now cover with a full, huge cross that bore the name of love. Values were unchanged. Numbers were simplified. One was one and that was all that was needed in a big world that had big numbers and big events. Two were one. Everything thereafter was brought down to one. And one was good. And two was good. Fractions were not needed. Decimals were in disarray. Debt was false. Future houses, future bills meant nothing compared to love. Unique were the moments. Math kept busying itself. But time was slowed. Love entered, stayed, and goodness came from it. The distinction was the moment. The true moment. Consistency made relevance a real word. Love brewing and pushing time back to zero and making all numbers possible in a world that really did not know much else worthy of trying to be obtained. Love. A higher math. Life without love, a primary arithmetic. A zero that grew as time went by.

But then, as love grew, the open spirit entered it and made freedom bloom from the frozen ground of the single life.

Love; you think you rest, and you do with love. Love. Your minds go into pieces and come back as one. All shattering the works of the day. But then building them up. You both know things now. The realm of hope is in each action. Palestrina, the Missa Breva, equal one; the kyries and the Sri Krishna and the Bible mean they are behind you: You two. You have love in your minds. You do love. You know love. Then, you have more love to give and more, to all and to each other. The ego and irony that are definitions in single life are dismissed as just words. You both wish to sit on a timeless beach and let the sun behave and let the waters wash over you and warm you with the sun in its mind, and you say love, love, love. You go to work and wonder and breathe. Bad things never obtain freedom within you. You fade into sleep in each other's arms and wake freshened and smile and kiss before you even shower. You have the world work for you. God, at times, needs your help to make those understand, who need to understand, that all things will turn out fine if love is included in the details. A child will see you smile. You have an infinite space to fill and paint. A child will be born of this, a single child, and all will be fine because you love yourselves, and him.

If You Traveled Around the Universe At The Speed Of Light, The Journey Would End Before You Got Back Home

*T*he facts about sound and hearing: Jim and Jane heard each other talking, even though it seemed it was from far away. Their sounds existed in two ways. They heard each other in actuality and potentiality. Some of their sounds were like sponges. Some like bronze bells. The two could produce sounds between themselves that were loud, and some as soft as a South American jungle wind. Their organs of hearing could make some sounds out rather strongly and others, well, they both felt like whispering, "Huh? Say again. Do again. Please."

Sometimes, Jim felt like the striker, other times, like the one to which a blow was struck. Such were the sounds of love in this Cleveland neighborhood. Yet, blows could never occur without movement. The two were moving. Time mattered when the chiming would begin. Everyone knows that afterwards, reverberation would be the discourse between their hearts. Air was all around. Escape possible, but not without the permission of the lover. The air, the water, the love. In the distance, a nun was heard singing singularly in Latin. The music was beautiful, even though only a few could hear it, and during this day and age, understand the lyrics. Truly understand the words and their intent.

Echoes of lightening are frightening. But only if those who hear them hear them close, maybe only a second away from them. Jane and Jim could hear the reverberations from minutes away, which seems like hundreds of miles away. Still, every sound was becoming closer and closer. Empowerment was closing in.

Joe Taylor from El Paso. On CNN. The dangerous noise continues. The sound of this ever-present copter. The blast of the sixteen-wheeler careening through the Texas countryside. The possible noise of what is going on in this man's head as he makes the decision to drive a stolen truck through the rugged terrain of Texas. The news here is brief. Nothing new to report. The man goes. He goes to where, no one knows. We will interrupt the current news to let you in on this journey through the suburbs of El Paso, Texas. Now back to our regularly scheduled broadcast...

The axis within Jane's body was happy. That first imaginary fight, long ago, had totally been forgotten. Jane was feeling younger than she was. Like many good things soon would be happening in her life. She said to no one in particular, but to everyone who knew love, "My life is happy." A smile came, "Tied within my robe is the faith that love will be what it will be. The knot is loose and will mean I will have freedom, and because of this, I will love him more than ever."

The season continued. It became mild. "I will see the good in him. The permanent good. I will throw away his flaws because in the long, long run, they will mean nothing to love. Ah, devotion, love and understanding." Even at night, the moon spoke to Jane, "All these abstract words roll from your tongue. They only mean nothing to those who have nothing. Everything is coming to you. Love. You have faith. You will obtain love. You will. Believe me, you will." To Jane, the moon always had a mild way to tell exciting news.

And Jane responded to the orb, "I have taken the right road. The free lane. And I have alit upon God. A good journey. My otherworldly knowledge will make me be devoted to Jim's love. I will trust him, even if he errs. Such an Adam will be with me in eternity. I am a patron of the heart. Love desire. I love love. I will be comfortable in his closeness of heart. His sweet lift of knots. I have faith in what will be."

This day, country music was playing in the background. The two kept hearing music. Neither of them knew where it was coming from. The sounds were sweet and soothing.

Jim cried about the egotism he owned, owned with a passion. He knew he must rid himself of most of it. It was like Lao-tzu was speaking to him through Christ. Both had quietly powerful voices: "The warmth of the cinnabar frees you. James, the point directs you to leave who you were. It is worthwhile to journey now. Yes, we will lament that you are leaving your old ways. You will see light, and all will be the love that is coming. The open love. The road will be the love. And this love will lead to everything. Everything good."

Jim did not respond other than to smile.

How can the human love meet the celestial kind? Jim was finding out, but he was not speaking about it. He knew he was not supposed to let these things loose. All was meant for everyone in its time. The winds would blow when spoken to. All would walk within the sky when they needed to. Holiness was never earned. Just happened. God was the stead. Jim was the steed.

Math did not enter this day. The sun, the one, was climbing and making it hard to see the glory. Its glare made the eyes avoid the truth of the moment. Time for work. Work did not require that much light. It's only saving grace.

Both walked around. Jim and Jane. Gifts were on the way. Until then, time meant a shaking of the trees as leaves fell and were blown away.

Ghostly patterns were not ones these two feared. The speed of light frolicked, and the journeys the two climbed onto would never end. And the true journeys would be perfect and yet real.

Both remembered dates they had as adolescents. Jim, the one in which all things went well. He took Lindy out; she was kind, beautiful, and loving. They saw a movie, The Wizard of Oz, and fell in love with it. They rent it to this day. Afterwards, they went to Burger Boy, each had a massive burger, and Jim drove her home. Lindy was short. Jim allowed her to climb up to the second step of her parents' house in Buckeye. And he kissed her lightly. She thanked him. She entered her home. And they never spoke again. And Jim never understood why and never asked and was always perplexed by the whole thing but was mostly perplexed because nothing happened, and there was no reason for nothing happening. Yet, everything felt well. Now, Jim realized why. Jim was supposed to meet Jane in middle age and be in love forever. He didn't notice he had a path then. When he was young.

And Jane remembered a time she asked a boy out, something that was not done in those days. The boy's name was Jim, not this Jim, but Jim Smith, like her last name, but from a different school. And this Jim said yes. Had no problems with the newness of this invitation. They went to a basketball game. Akron U was playing Cleveland State in a gym near their homes. They sat in the bleachers like everyone else. Except, Jane tried to kiss this other Jim and he said no. That that would lead to sex. The other Jim quietly spoke, "I was taught not to kiss until marriage, not to even hold hands. I think my parents are right about this. They told me to go out with you because I should be nice. And I responded, 'Yes Mom, that I will do.' And here I am, doing the right thing. Is that okay?"

Jane said, "Yes, this is good." She never called this other Jim after their date. She forgot about him. Until now. Now, she remembered the reasons why things occur. And she remembered that she should not speak about those reasons. And she did not.

And life went on. Neither one of these two would tell their little stories to each other. Never.

In The Past The Distance Between Galaxies Was Zero

*I*n the archaeology of the moment, the two were always one. Evidence has always existed that love was there eons ago. Lying in a grave somewhere. One lady had on a necklace. The other, a dull man, had a ring in his nose. The tableland gave them away. Their grave was heightened by their ancestors. You could tell there was trouble with their only kid. She laid down a ways from them in the mound, about ten feet from them. The two who were very close to each other. She was by his side, except for the baby that lie five feet from her. He was almost touching her. The quiet of the moment was thousands of years old.

The man had one of his bony arms wrapped around his wife. There was a smile cemented onto his skull.

Their sex was one. The two in today's world, Jane and Jim, dreamed. Suspense and love are endless. Each time different. Each better. Each time, at times, a problem. Most of the time there were no concerns. Some lovers are into constant analysis. Others just consider the next time. And that love is there and has little to do with sex. Love is a mountain. Sex, foothills. Epistemology, figures, and the other sciences of the orgasm all dream in irrational sequences that appear to be nothing. Jane had an insuperable necessity. Without Jim, she touched herself each evening before bed, and dreamed of the beauties inherent in lovemaking. Jim scratched himself in the morning in the shower, and that made him start his day. He did that with Jane and without Jane. With love in truth, or with love as a cosmetic, love has its glorious times, times that cannot be simply written about in books. Jim and Jane were writing their story without words, phrases, and paragraphs. Time described the intensity of their desires. Time was the only one that knew of their confidences.

Freud brought ruptures. A scientist who knew way too much. Too much thought. Too much disseminating. Too much movement. And, of course, more psychiatrists with their drugs. Too many psychologists with their words. Not enough privacy. The culture knows way too much about itself. And the culture never deals with all the knowledge anyway.

Jane said, "Sex is a group of objects that should not be talked about it." Jim said he agreed. "Let the scientists get sick while we smile about them. I suppose that is mean." Jane said it was. Jim was in love and agreed. Both smiled at how the days were warming up. How the coldness was changing to intermittent warmth. How, even at night, it was warm enough to wear sweaters and be happy. How it was getting warm enough at night to sleep in the nude. Both spoke, "Ah…" to each other.

A Common Loon shot down like a cannon ball to the lone pond in their neighborhood. The little lake had no name. Both saw it for a few days. Both had not seen each other yet. The Loon lasted for two weeks. The Loon left for Ontario, some large unnamed lake in the upper reaches of the province. In order to find his mate. The loon knew the lady was there. To swim about, to duck into the weeds to obtain fish, to swim deeper and for longer periods in the summer to find fish and test his lungs, to give the fish to his baby as his wife watched and did some of the work herself, and how they remained together to give to the young. The male was coloring himself as he edged north. Such are love and birds.

Consequences unspoken. Jim's expressions were equivalent to identical thoughts inside of his numb skull. Jane's were equal to one and the same. No math intended. They retraced steps, took algebraic letters and reduced them, reached for the equal sign, dismissed every past equation ever learned, subtracted/added and then multiplied/divided and then looked at all the answers and do not worry much over them because love was the final answer.

Love present and exact. Jim and Jane simultaneously thought of autonomy. God dismissed the theories in their heads. God knew there was more to life than ideas.

All in the real world tends to corrupt love. Jim was reminded of a time he dated a pretty lady in college. A date he was set up with by his friends. Girlfriends.

She was beautiful, and she was brown. He went over her house to pick her up to take her to a cheap movie, one of those dollar flicks, second run but good. College kids and the lack of cash and the Jeans that last for years with holes in them and how they looked even better then. Because the body was beautiful and looked good with rags on. Jim had a pocketknife in his Jacket.

Linda's dad went to get their coats after meeting Jim and shaking his hand and seeing he was a nice boy, and then he felt the pockets of Jim's coat just because the old man was employed by the Cleveland Police Department, and that was the way he was. The father felt a pocketknife in the jacket, came from the bedroom, where the jacket lay on the parents' bed, and told his daughter that she would not be able to go on her date with Jim. He used those words. Linda did not ask why. She immediately went to her room. The father then showed the knife to Jim. And Jim, knowing that the father was a cop, said nothing and left, without his date or his knife.

The knife got thrown away in the garbage. Such is sometimes the way love is. More questions than answers. Too difficult to understand.

Jane remembered a time when her father said no to a date at that instant of Jim's memory. Similarities exist in all the lives on the whole planet.

This autonomy continued. Everyone on earth has a lamp within their minds. All there is left is to light it. Fathers do this at one time in their youths before they are fathers. Mothers do this when they are mothers. Fathers, sons, daughters and wives become immortal.

Jane was beautiful her whole life. Her father knew what he was facing as his daughter aged. Boys with penises. And big ambitions. A boy came to pick Jane up to walk her to a football game in the late fall. The temperatures were starting to dip. Mr. Smith met the boy in his driveway and told him to get his ass home. The boy asked why. Mr. Smith punched him one time in the stomach and the boy heaved his dinner. Mr. Smith went to get a bucket of water to dilute the old supper around the browning grasses of the neighbor's house. Then he said to the boy again to get his butt home, don't go to the game or come over again. The boy agreed and did not say another word as he disappeared into the void that was the night in the city. The father came back into the house.

Mr. Smith reported to his daughter that he just happened to meet her date as he was going out for a walk, and that the boy told him that he could not take Jane to the game, that she should go herself or with her friends. Jane said nothing and went up to her room to get another sweater and some gloves for the game. As she was coming back down the steps, she told her father that she needed more cloths to keep warm for the big game. Her father agreed and smiled. Jane smiled. End of story.

Fathers discriminate all the time without good reasons for the action. The conditioning of a daughter flares them up. The confusion in the thoughts meant nothing in the long run. The distance between parents and children are immense and close at the same time. Parental love has nothing to do with love. Only with safety and ownership. And keeping things on a string. After a long while, many parents think this is love. It takes a good parent to understand that love is different from parenting. If parents would practice pure love with their mates, they would understand the differences in the word love.

Jim has a photo. He is four. He has on a cheap imitation of Hopalong Cassidy's chaps, the cowboy's hat, and a plaid shirt; one toy gun and a cheap holster. His mom is in the far background and looks worried about life. Like death is permanent and will happen to her boy. Like there is not enough food in the house. Like the mom and dad have just come out of a depression. Like bad girls live in the neighborhood. Like Jim will get bad grades in school. Like the cosmos is finite and will close in on the family and kill every kid, even the ones that were just considered but were never born.

There is a bright sun behind the mother. The boy has pride in his face. The mother is thinking he should not have pride. Pride worries her. She is desperately trying to make Jim feel dumb. She succeeds for a long time.

Jim is feeling that he will be hugged by beauty if he holds his pose long enough.

The gun, the holster, and the TV show make Jim feel like everything is worth fighting for. And that he will win if he tries to fight. Mothers do not like this scenario.

In the end, everyone will be happy.

Horses and Jim are going after outlaws, and catching them, and how the outlaws deserve to be hung. And there are no questions about any of this.

Someone said cheese, maybe a neighborhood lady during the middle of the day when dad was at work, and only Jim smiled. Mothers only smile when things are in their control. Most things with boys are not. Worries make everyone live longer. Things equal. Even though, the TV people will be back to ask dumb questions like, "Was he bad when he was young? Did you know he would rob banks and kill innocent people when he was on his bottle? And speaking of bottles, when did he start to drink too much?" TV people don't have much of any intelligence to speak.

TV people left. Everyone laughs when they die. And life is about mothers being hurt. No matter how good their kids are or become.

And the sun keeps screaming down from the depths of an ethereal sky that is cloudy often in Buckeye. The neighborhood is near Lake Erie. Still, its warmth is felt throughout the insulation of nature. And that is fine. Everything is fine.

Aristotle could read. His mother never found this out because she could not read. There are many things mothers do not know. But when they find out they accept them immediately and smile.

Jim and Jane were falling in love with time. Time was a mother they could love because it was innocent of caring.

Quantum Mechanics
Are About Randomness

*A*lways work the next day. And the next day. The next and... Jim walked to his car. Spring was arriving slowly. He heard a sound. At first, he thought it was his future lover's call from the sky, a sky this morning that was as blue as a Patagonian inlet experiencing another summer season. One Jim had seen photos of after Chatwin's travel book had come out years before.

A Cerulean Warbler sang his warm song through the few trees. Yes, unusual to see such a bird in this Buckeye neighborhood. Such a bird was used to the woods of a true country life, not the cold, narrow houses of the inner city. Jim's eyes wished to see this male, slightly smaller than his hand, sitting on a phone wire, singing a song of tiny, warbled notes short and sweet as a slight breeze among a copse. Its high-pitched buzz was not being used. Jim said, "Go now to a clean river and sing your minute tempest. You brought me love this fine, late winter morning. You are she. She is you. I am your lover. You, a messenger of the ongoing movie that has been appearing in my dream life for decades." With the words, the warbler, after its long flight from Bolivia, pushed off the wire and made its way north to Jane's home. Jim got in his vehicle and left for work.

By her true nature, Jane always desired to know. The lady's senses were full and always open to the world. She loved sight above all others. On her way to her work, she spotted love. Jane was sensing it was coming.

A car in front of her had a man and a woman going to work sitting next to each other. Not apart like old married folks. Jane thought that this was a sign that she should sit next to Jim regardless of how many years they remained married, no matter how many fights they would have, and no matter how many children came into their marriage. Jane said to herself, "I will love Jim when I have the chance. I will not dismiss him ever as baggage. When we have time together, I will touch him with my fingers, my body, and my mind and my soul. Nothing should ever get in my way of expressing my love for Jim." Jane's sense of sight was acute. The lady brought her arm up and put it around her lover's broad shoulders. He turned his head and Jane could see he had a smile on his rugged face, made a funny comment and his sweet wife smiled right back. And that was that. A sign on the way to work that love was brewing in two lives. Metaphysics were flying. Their sights were bringing warmth to the relationship. The one that had not brought its reality to these city scenes.

Always there are thoughts. The floating realms of warmth came to the two simultaneously. Every action ought to show respect for life. A smile would show they were warm about each other, that there were not others in the past, or would there be new loves in the future. Love had come into two lives and respect for the egos of each to each would always be shown. Jane and Jim felt this about each other.

The hands. Jim would love his future wife's hands, the sight of them, their touch, and then, he would put his rough hands into hers and that would be part of their love making: The touch of their hands. The music would play. The song would be a slow song, one of tough touching souls finding their routes to glory. The hands. Jim knew that each time he would touch his wife, that Jane would smile. All in synchronous motion, all alive as the rare birds that would fly into their lives, and the songs that would be song to show them that they had attained God's rarest gift. Jim felt he would never allow enter from his life anything that would frighten Jane. All things, all live would be about true love.

Random words were now coming into the heads of the two as they made their ways to work. Jane: "He will be the prism through which the light of day will be changed for me. More colors will be blazing in my life. No other company will have ever done this for me." Jim: "I was rather a timid boy. Now, with Jane coming, I will feel like a full-blown flower that deserves, finally, to be plucked. Smiles of love will always be upon my face. I will nothing else other than my Jane. Yes, life will be enjoyable. It always has been. But with Jane it will be an everlasting party."

More. From Jane, "Me too. Once nervous and self-conscious, I will see him and know that what I say to him will always be correct."

"She! I thought that with my sad childhood I would come out as an old, dried weed. Now that I have her, I feel the life of a strong, every growing tree. Still, I will feel just right. I will not arrogate one touch of superiority to her."

"It is incumbent upon me to show a noble life. I will know my love for him will end of any foolishness I have within me." We will have upright hearts. Morality, decency, and clean living will be our hallmarks. With subtlety, we will show our rawness to our families and friends so they will know we have not gone Victorian. Our American spirits will blossom along with our love. You, my Jim, will be my poet."

"You, my Jane, will be my poet. A letter better - our hearts in a true place."

"I will laugh at you, and with you, and the sounds still will carry love to your heart of hearts."

"Jane, sweet, sweet Jane."

After work, Jim got in his car and wrote a note to Jane.

Dear Jane,

I love thee. But I must tell you something about me. I must confess who I am. Dante wrote, "Que s'asconde mel velame degli nodi strani..." He said... hiding in the veil of the strange knots is... well, well... LOVE.

I cannot tell you everything sad and heavy in my life. I will not. But it is there. I have been on evil journeys, some set by myself, other brought to me. I can only ask your forgiveness.

Why, you ask. The rooms are so small they are not worth the ventures. I know the rooms are still there. They are powerful. The rooms are many in my life. Poor ideas, poor faith, poor loves, poor imperfections, a poor God. I brought all into my life, and I ask for your love and forgiveness in one giant stroke. I am happy to leave the small rooms. Yes, others have large, ornate rooms. Ones that are full of total evil. I promise I will be able to leave whatever rooms I have and lead a clean life, one with straight hallways that always lead to you and your soft touch.

And what the devil does is his business. I will be with God and you forever as one entity.

I will walk away like I have the bad paintings in the museum, knowing they have affected me, but knowing also that I have straightened and aligned my future to be yours.

I know these are like vows. I do say them in front of God. I promise to have a happy face when I am with you. I will perform happy deeds. I will touch you with my simple fingers and give you my tender love.

Love, Jim

This is CNN! I break into the regularly scheduled news to tell you nothing, I repeat that NOTHING is happening in this adventure I brought you an hour ago. That is exactly an hour ago. A man, who is nameless, has hijacked a truck near El Paso, has proceeded east, away from the city, and now is going back to the city, and he is driving very fast on Motana-Lockheed Road, Route 62/180, will be coming into Ciudad Juarez, and looks like he wants to get home, west into El Paso again. What his intents are is anyone's guess. Fortunately, no one has been injured by his ventures. Lives have luckily been spared. However, there have been some close calls. Right now, at this moment we are seeing a close call. Oh My God. Oh My God---The massive eighteen-wheeler has just went through a four way stop sign and barely missed a fruit truck. A fruit truck full of kumquats. Wow! What can I say? Now, back to your regularly scheduled news show on CNN. This is Joe Taylor reporting...

A bunch of 'yeses' come in love. Jane was one of the few girls in her literature class in high school to finish Joyce's Ulysses. The final stream of consciousness scene when the positive word is spoken many times was always in Jane's head. Yes. That was how marriage was coming out for her. Yes. The good word with no evil attached, like in many relationships. Yes, I will, yes, say yes, always to you. Yes. A yes-kind-of-love!

"We are love. We speak the word because it is a gift. We are not deluded by our emotions. We know there is an essence. Ordinary ignoramuses we are not. We are special ones, why, because we have love. We are love. The senseless vacuity of life is away from us. We will not give huge pleasure to shopping anymore. We will not spend hours watching dumb TV. We will give a hoot about good weather shows or bad weather shows. We will see each other's eyes and know they have more sense in them than sight. We are love. One. And, oh, what a gift that is given to us by God.

The math of love seeps in. We will meet, finally meet, and we will see. All the theorems will be one. There will be a completeness and a consistency that will overwhelm us over the years. Unification. Proofs will comprise peace. A quiet will come. A justification of a primary arithmetic will arrive. A one plus one plus one. Indicators of the perfect love will state that we are distinguished by the first distinction. Contractions will disappear. Tiny theorems will go away. Our gate of entry will be a new calculus. A connection." The two were speaking in dreams as one. The unity was the word we.

Jim and Jane thought, "All will give rise to new theorems invented by our friends and family." Old logisms will be spoken, "Look at this mature couple, in love. Wow!" And, "I did not think they would ever find love. Now, I am Jealous that their love is above the meaning I had derived from love. I envy them. Although I know I should not. God does not like us to envy his unique visions. He wants us to pray that somehow we might have a bit of the gift."

Like two calculi have become one. The mixed theorems have dissolved into a cosmos that is beyond the infinite. Ah. Love. Ah. Jim and Jane and an utter uniqueness. An indefinable power. A thrust towards the heavens.

One fellow, a worker at the gas station Jane always frequented said, "She was just another random customer. Now, she has sun in her eyes."

Einstein said,
"God Does Not Play Dice!"

*L*ove, what is love, Love or love or LOVE? It comes. It goes. Today, love comes.

Believe love or not. Just feel it. Jim and Jane believe it, because they believe love. They have felt it coming all these years. Yes, they both knew love was coming. At 8:02am today on March 20 in the year 2002, will be an historic moment in their lives. The brief instant will not be marked by the chiming of any bells, but at that precise time on this specific date in our world's history, something will happen that has not happened in the roughly forty-five years, give or take a few, of their middle-aged lives. Still, what we are gabbing about is love. Love happened for these two in the years before. Love will happen during this time they find each other. They will date, have a brief engagement, marry, live and pass on. Simple yet unbelievable.

As the clock ticks past 8:01 am on this Wednesday, time will, for sixty seconds read a perfect symmetry, or to be more precise, this moment will never have the same poignancy as the eleventh hour of the eleventh day of the eleventh month which marks a kind of non-Armistice Day of Hate. Love will continue as it always continues. Hate will fade, as it was meant to do in the crush of mankind. Time will do away with hate. Love will reign as it was meant to when God created it.

Words versus love in early spring. Jim's drying looks will bring perfect thoughts to his rattled mind. Hard dreams of the way love should be will reside between the old buildings in Buckeye. Love will be here like the first robin of the season. The bird's orange chest will fill Jim's eyes. Jim will watch the robin search for places he could never find. But now the male will find them. The old bird looks over to Jim and looks like it is bored with him. Like the robin knows he has been searching for love without a heart. Jim has read tomes and tomes about love, but he never let the words leave him so that he could find love's heart. Jim pleads to make words flow from him. Even, in this moment, he does not understand that he should let God put the words in his mouth about love, not books.

A cardinal enters his view. This bird has been here all winter. The Cardinal dashes in flight from a maple tree to an oak to a dead neighbor's, cherry tree. The huge cherry knew this man was in love when he passed at a ripe age to a land with a name that did not mean a thing at this time in his life. Jim thought, "I can no longer run from tree to tree looking. It is my time to find. I will let myself find love. It is my time."

"My core is with love. I will move fluently with love's ideas of being alive. I am starting to smell the odor of being with death too much. Death no longer frightens me. Seeking God's positive love, I see being's love in the seconds of the future. I felt like the sparrows, who I now see darting from seed to seed, nervous and alive, but lacking the depth of the beautiful fowl. With love near, I am not common anymore. The sparrows are tossing away, with their nervous habits, my meaningless movements. I wonder what Jane is doing now."

A=a. b=b. a+b=c, an unknown that is known. A gift that is spoken about often, but in which the depth is never fully understood in a huge world that passes it by to find things. Things more comfortable than c. c too much to try and truly understand. Indexing, justification, replacements, values and more values, rules, theorems, consequences, the primary arithmetic leads to the primary algebra. Love, the higher form of math is way beyond any concept in math. The one we have never taken in and kept and lived with every second of our existence. Love, math, the same. One is the best though.

The secret of every flower. The consciousness of one is enough to most. Purity and impurity. Most go for the impurity of it. They are afraid to touch the perfection, so they immediately make it dirty, go after others who have the same values, touch them with their dirty hands and dirty thoughts, and smile because they have corrupted love and brought it down to their level. The lesser Christ went to the desert to find a reed. One that bends with the winds that seem to constantly blow. Those around him kept asking, "What did you go to the desert to find?" He said a reed. He said you may think I found the wind, or the blueness of the sky, or a waft of love. He said it is not my purpose to find these. He said you must find those. He said I have found the reed. The reed is the prophet. Not I, he said. He said you trust in me, and you will find more. Much more.

Jane entered the morning with a laugh. A funny dream about work the night before was lingering. She said a bunch of things to herself, "I am a worker."

She continued speaking in jolts in the shower, "I am trying to be a hero."

"I work to sweat. I am no hero."

"I endow my fine body to search for him. And, as always, myself."

"I only bring my muscles along to search for pain."

"I wish to see the truth of love as I exult in pain in a woman's wish for perfection."

"All the love."

"All the love is coming."

"To make my soul perfect, I must work it. Work for it."

"I must seek what I need this day."

"I will find love."

"Today."

'My body, my mind, must become godly to find love."

"Today is love's day."

"I will cry when I find it."

"I have needed to grind out the hours without love."

"Now, I see love coming."

Jane thought, "Clean love is one form of the good life. I will show nothing to Jim that will frighten him. In the past, in his mind, I already did that. It was like a test. He still loved me. Now, I will show him that I will never test him again. I will show him there will be never any conditions that will keep my love for him. Unconditionally, I will ever be with him."

Jim said to himself, "Love is a pair of we humans per acre."

Jim went out to his car to go to work. He heard singing before he opened the driver side door. The singing was beautiful. It was not from any car radios in the neighborhood. During the winter many folks on his street started their cars, to get them warm before they headed to their labors. On this early spring day, the sun was shining. It was a cloudless sky. Most were going to work in sweaters. Early spring. The tempest of winter was finished.

"You are beautiful today." Jim had words in his mouth that were flowing out of his self. At first, they were murmurs. Jim's voice kept strengthening.

Jim felt that the music seemed to be coming from the street that bordered his. The music was from Notre Dame, the avenue that ran parallel to his. It was a voice he had not heard before. A lady's voice. Jim could not tell if it was alto, soprano, or... He was not even willing to understand the exact words, or from what opera the sounds were emanating. Jim felt the music was for him. He felt that the love behind the sound was to be his.

Jim did not get into his car. Jim did not go to work this morning.

Jane was approaching her vehicle. She was thinking a banal thing; was glad she did not have to scrape the frost from the windshield. Jane was feeling ready. Jane was totally stopped in her driveway. She was not moving. No one was noticing any of this. Jane knew she was of another color. She knew Jim was of another color. Now, she was seeing one perfect color. The color of spring. Jane wished to say, "You are beautiful. You are beautiful." Yet, she knew it was not time.

Jane walked across the street. To her, this moment, this street did not feel like a church. God had not felt like he was here ever before. Now all was changed. Holy was the love that Jane was feeling now. A moment, now. Jane walked up a sidewalk then took a left and headed up a driveway and crossed a lot to another driveway and then down that driveway to the next street. But she was stopped before she got there.

Time elapsed. The two did not know it had. The two were in love.

Jim was there, right in front of her. In love. His eyes showed every speck of love. With all his might he wanted to shout out that he was in love. Jim did not. The time was not right.

Jim was exactly six feet tall. Brown hair, brown eyes. A mole on his cheek. A ruddy complexion. No hat. His hair was combed perfectly after his morning shower. Jim looked in shape. Jane was showing good youth. No one would think she was in her forties. Not how most spinsters looked. Because she had been traveling life knowing love was at her door. Jane had brown hair and eyes. Long hair. Flowing hair. And, no hat on. Light color spring clothes. A blue belt around her thin waist. She was also a walker like Jim. A fruitful bosom. A constant smile on her soft face.

Church bells rang. Seven times. St. Andrews small Catholic church three streets over was coming to life this glorious morning.

Jane said, "I know you, don't I?"

"I have always known you."

Jane, "I... I want to know more about you, but I am afraid that I will never truly understand you. Still, I wish to try."

"I know you are there. This is all I have ever prayed for. I... love you." Jim was crying. Jane was crying. It was their lives crying together. The tears were perfect tears because they were good tears. Love and tears mixed as one with a liquid as quiet as space.

Love was coming. "I... love you. I have always loved you. Deep dreams I have had. The good ones have always been about you. The good ones have been about love."

Jim whispered, "We had a fight. We will never have another. Forever."

"I know. God has spoken to me."

"No work this day."

"No work."

"Love."

"Love."

The sun was rising above the house tops. Warmth was coming into the congested neighborhood. Jim was thinking the words Notre Dame had a different meaning for him. But not one of ownership. One of love. Jane was considering all the time. That time was the time that was love. And how everything was changing in her life in this moment. The moment she knew was coming. Still, the reality made every sense to her. Jim and Jane. And love. And love. And love.

What Matters Is Continuous

A warm wind blew the view of spring into Jim and Jane's lives. A concrete love was upon their table. Erratic lives were coming into a oneness that was beyond any perfect description.

All this bliss on the day before Jim had found out his VCR had taped a nothing event on CNN that had happened days before. He had not read about the eighteen-wheeler in the newspapers. So, he knew his recorder had not come upon anything of any importance to the history of the planet. Yet, he enjoyed watching the non-event two minutes at a time appearing on his large-screen TV. Past news about nothing intrigued him. In his way, he was making fun of the millions spent to find one person doing something out of the ordinary in the American world. His sarcasm was balanced by the fact he was trying to find the reasons for nothing making breaking news. "Ah, the rewards of silly chaos," he thought.

Again, this is CNN, Jim Taylor, and breaking news from El Paso, Texas. The massive eighteen-wheeler with the man who is still unidentified, continues on its march to El Paso. Steady, the truck is traveling, we estimate, at around forty miles an hour. One mailbox has been shattered, but no victims as of yet in this terrible tragedy. Is this about a lonely man looking for company? Or is this about an evil one looking for destruction? We shall see. And we shall keep in touch with the scene and give you updates on what is occurring here in the deepest South of our great country. Just one aside. He has gone through two red lights. The cops are still on his tail, sirens blazing. Again, this is Joe Taylor of CNN. We will keep you informed...

Jim was now considering touch. He heard those three words that every man wants to hear every day of his life. Jim was now looking forward to the touch of her fingers and the first kiss. A light and loving kiss in which he wanted to send the message of his good, trustworthy heart to Jane.

That night, promptly at six, he made another walk, one that traveled straight to her house on Notre Dame. He knocked on her door. The place had been renovated. Jim looked inside and saw that everything was neat and ordered. Jane was walking inside, making her way to the kitchen. Then she heard her front door and knew who it was. Jane came to the door. Jim had a smile on his face before she even unlocked it. A peace was descending and elevating him and his spirit.

"Hi, good day?" And he lightly kissed her. And his eyes looked into hers, and she saw that he did have a good day and Jane said, "I did. And I see you also had a good one at work." Jim smiled a smile that was full of warmth. Jane noticed he was content, and her smile that she produced back to Jim was full of innocence and deep love. The love in a fourteen-year-old girl. Jane was forty-two in this spring of a year she would always remember. The light feeling of real love was entering her life and making her understand the true meanings of two who live on an 'Eden' called earth. That the ultimate gift one can give to another is a life. Not her house, her car, her long hours making big money at work, not her clean doilies, not her fresh food bought at the local grocery store that day before she got home from her career, and not her clean history of waiting for the right man to knock at her door.

Jane was special like every other woman that walked the countryside and the city. She observed love coming. She felt it as it arrived. And she knew that its length was eternal, no matter what the vows of marriage stated. The death till you part phrase she knew meant nothing to the sweetness and length of Jim's love for her. The Gaia of God's moments with her were totaling in a timeless way.

A lone male Cardinal was perching outside Jane's door. He seemed to be looking in. His stout, red bill was pointing at the two. His "what-cheer, cheer, cheer!" kind of voice was pronouncing the joy of the moment. The male had been looking around for chips and twigs and leaves and plant fibers to make a nest in a neighborhood thicket. It was like his lady knew that he was different, that she was not going to have to do all the work, and that he was more than a man doing work to take up time. That he understood about love. That made him a bit different from the masses of men who had come to her door. That this bird's red robes were not just color. That a good Catholic Cardinal knows about the love of man, the good side, and not just the segments that bring headlines to foolish newspapers. That this bird sang year round, love lived for what it truly was, not the workings of pitying crowds of sarcastic men and their dull voices. This Cardinal, a member of the finch family had a wonder that included his workings with those he found special. The bird looked into Jane's window and saw that things were going fine. Jane felt his thoughts deeply within her spring.

The two were feeling love's hugeness. Both could not see all the words that mean love, but they were feeling them simultaneously in their lives. Love was becoming the nature of their whole. And that love was infinite in its delicate size. Love was capable of locomotion. That it is the soul principle of pure movement. The straight and circular lines that lead to love are both fine because of where they end up. Jane and Jim had been attached to the circular route. Patience had been the key. God had given that strength to view these figures. Now, things were simplifying. The center of love was good. Quickly, Jane and Jim were entering this zone, and they were ready for it. Three dimensions had been achieved. The fourth was in view and the vastness of the fourth did not frighten these two. As individuals they had walked in this dimension for years, both surrendering to a perfect God early in their maturities.

Sure, Jane and Jim had gnawed their nails, shook their heads, leaned on wrongheaded people, played with angry fires, slept when others spoke, yawned at their own private matters, and frightened their friends with their awful tales of life. They had gone through those periods when folks show nasty attention to their ineptitudes. Life was meaning more now. The poetry of it was now showing the worth of love. Before love had come, poetry was bombastic language that meant nothing to winners. At this point, winners to them were not whole until they found love.

Their conversation was continuing, "Couldn't wait to come and see you! Have a good day?"

"I love you Jim."

"I have waited patiently for you. You are here. Have always been here. Now, I have found you. And can touch you. I love you."

"I will not let those three words slip from my vocabulary."

"Neither will I."

"The two of us have history. We know love. We shall not allow our love to get in the way of our lives. Neither we allow our lives to get in the way of our love for each other."

"It is like we are saying our vows this moment. And we are. But we also say them in front of a God who understands and pushes our every move."

"Yes."

"Yes, with his glory."

"That word will bring us of all the buildup in our lives of tough sites, and tough sounds, and the rigors of moving in a disturbed world."

"I love thee."

"I would love to give you a light kiss. Passion will come later. And we are not afraid of that, are we!?"

"You understand." Jane and Jim. Their lips. Wet. The warm moistness of the future was bonding in their movement, a leaning together as they stood, and then, a parting as their eyes met, they combined their two meanings into bliss.

Jane thought, "It is not the man who sits by his fireside reading the evening paper and saying to himself how bad the world is who will ever do anything to bring love to a woman. It is the man who goes out into the narrow, hurly-burly caucus of Buckeye life and faces misery and equals it that draws me to him. It is Jim. He is not aloof. Takes chances. Survives because he has a deep history of knowing the strengths of love. I will always love his blood, his sweat. And he me." And Jim thought, "She is my ever-beauty! I have been allowed to digress. Now, my good work begins. A work I look forward to. Jane. I will keep our love strong. This son of a Christian will plea for her health to a God who listens. I will tell others I have changed because of a beautiful lady."

Kisses, light ones, continued. The night brought them to a moment of breaking up and going to their rest. Their heads, they used them. Harmony was showing all over the neighborhood. It always does early in relationships. Yes, testing would occur. But they knew they would pass those anxious moments with flying colors.

The seed of love had fallen from the all the greening trees of Cleveland life.

The soil was good. The weather was temperate and bringing spring. The stalk was growing just as they knew it would grow, bringing a full life all around. Jane and Jim knew much. And much was coming to them. The fruit was love. That is what was needed in their equations. Simple equations. Simple math wrought the complexities of undying love and made their equations perfect and alive in one instant.

Love Divides And
Multiplies Without Limit

"*I* told her I loved her. I kissed Jane. It's like I meant that I have both commodities to give without limit. This is the way love should feel. It is." His head was again thinking in terms of love. Jim's walk home in the dark brought his head up so his eyes could gaze at the clearing sky. A full moon was rising in the west. Its large presence was making his see the wonders that God provides for him. Those words he sometimes said openly were bouncing off the glitter of the moon. The houses in Buckeye seemed like castles. This knight in his day's work-clothes felt the warmth of love's safety, of love's hearth. Jim's big life was becoming full and glorious. Normal times were disappearing in the gray darkness of this little neighborhood's idle corners.

"I must pray. The prayer must be one of thanks." In the middle of Notre Dame Ave. this middle-aged man got down on his knees in the dank blackness of this early spring evening and looked up and whispered a few words. At the end of his message he shouted, "Father, I am with you. I am with you. I will always be with you. I wish to whisper, 'Thank you.' A few words and immense feeling about the gift you have given me, her! Jane is me. I am her. You have brought us together. You told us you would.

Thanks. Thank you for you, and thank you for Jane, and thank you for bringing love into my regular life. Love. Love... LOVE!" The neighborhood slept. No one heard the colossal word. Yet, a few who knew love for the gift it had given them smiled as they watched TV or went to bed or brushed their teeth or as they read a book or the newspapers or took into their bodies a late snack or as they pondered the meaning of our immense world and its troubles. They felt the word love, and it made things well for them. They didn't know why they felt a warmth in their lives. The chosen heard the loudly spoken word and felt its infinite touch.

The word produced much. Love multiplied, always multiplied, and flew in various directions like the chaos of hate but in a much more soothing manner. During the spotting of love all else is put away. Including desperate hate. And love would win. Some even realized it was winning now. As years floated above Jane and Jim, the ache that is hate would unreel at tiny times. And hurt loosened a bit. But love, the great blanket it provides, would conquer pain. LOVE shouted once on a dark street that was named after a loving mother. Would its good shivers flow down the back of a nation that knew it for its perfect freedom?

Jane readied herself for bed. She possessed the book she was reading, a warm shower, a brushing of her teeth, a CD playing Horowitz's romantic ideas of Mozart, and the white, fluffy filled blanket on her double bed.

Jane began to talk to herself, "He is mine. He is fine. My life feels sublime. It is our time. We will hear the bells chime. I feel, God, he is kind. And I am seeing now how the globe and all its inhabitants rhyme." She giggled at her foolishness. Crawled into bed, felt the softness of the sheets. Ran her lovely, long fingers through the strands of her hair. Smiled a warm smile. Looked up at the broad ceiling that was in her bedroom and gave a simple whisper of the word thanks.

Ah, another day tomorrow. And Jane was not thinking about work and its lunacies. She was considering the various textures of love. All of them and how love makes little things seem good and big. And big things better. And that others would view her the next day and take from her love's bangles, as she would freely give them out, and they would not necessarily know the gifts they were getting, but they would spot the smiles, and feel fine. And life would go on in a whirl of hope.

A Quark Has An Infinitely Simple Flavor Produced From All The Colors

"Ah, the complexities of our love." Jim cried at night before he slept. The sleep was deep. Love added to the digs. Alive, Jim felt each minute his body took in the peaceful dwellings the earth gave to him. Each morning he awoke he called his loved one.

"Hello Jane, a good night of sleep?"

"Yes... I love you."

"I love you. Please walk over to my place tonight. I will have dinner waiting for you."

"I will be there."

"My heart will be with you the entire day"

"And mine with yours each night." Such is the magnanimous charm of the moments, the words of love between Jane and Jim and their new life. Jim lived the life of the Bible verse, II Corinthians, about love, backwards or forwards, the verse was always good. Often, the verse came to him the wrong way, and it meant beauty. Jim felt that love was God's gift to him whether it was amid good times or confusing times. Love was beauty. Beauty, love. His understanding was growing for Jane. Jim felt the time was coming where they should talk of marriage together and how that should be. He whispered those words from the Bible as he drove to work, backwards,

"Tongues in speaking. Cymbal clanging a or gong resounding a only am I, love not have but, angels of and men of tongues the in speak I if. Nothing am I, love not have but, mountains move can that faith a have I if and, knowledge all and mysteries all fathom can and prophecy of gift the have I if. Nothing gain I, love not have but, flames the to body my surrender and poor the to possess I all give I if.

Kind is love, patient is love. Proud not is it, boast not does it, envy not does it. Wrongs of record no keeps love, angered easily not is love, self-seeking not is love, rude not is love. Truth the with rejoices but evil in delight not does love. Perseveres always, hopes always, trusts always, protects always love.

Fails never love. Away pass will it, knowledge is there where; stilled be will they, tongues are there where; cease will they, prophecies are there where but. Disappears imperfect the, comes perfection when but, part in prophesy we and part in know we for. Child a like reasoned I, child a like thought I, child a like talked I, child a was I when. Me behind ways childish put I, man a became I when. Face to face see shall we then; mirror a in as reflection poor a but see we now. Known full am I as even, fully know shall I then; part in know I now.

Love and hope, faith: remain three these now and. Love is these of greatest the but.

Jim and love. Inside of his heart, the sweet charms of love bred more love. Jim thought, "Anyone who speaks in tongues does not speak to me, but to God. 'God to but me to speak not does tongues in speaks who anyone.' But now, brothers, if I come to you and speak in tongues what good will I be to you, unless I bring you some revelation? Or love? Let us 'love have, you who over watch.' Get out of the way of love for us for too dumb to have problems your." Jim began to laugh in his car, alone. He felt he could. He knew he was being foolish, and he knew that God would feel that was okay as long as he did his insanity alone for this moment. Jim thought that this type of insanity brought on God's laughter because the fine one knew that the two would be closer to him, that they might even feel his deepest truths.

His confused backward words continued to ring out in his vehicle, "But still, with anger the or not which not we know is sin, and ask we forgiveness, we wish you love of trinity the and other love with other souls who love, much love, simple love, love, honest... love, yes, just love, love, love..." Jim had a smile on his face. It lasted him the day because it reached far into his utter soul.

Again and again, this is CNN, this is Joe Taylor, and this is the continuing story of a possible tragedy in Texas. The man, the truck. The massive eighteen-wheeler and possible death. But nothing of a terrible nature has occurred yet. I am up in our copter and we are watching the scene, traveling west towards El Paso where the traffic gets more frantic and many lives are in peril. Ah, we will watch, but nothing is happening yet. This unidentified man continues, missing pedestrians, hitting only a few stop signs and ditches...More news will be coming on CNN... We will keep you informed... Again, this is Joe Taylor and CNN news....

Jane was considering her heart. The traffic was down. It was a Friday, and many were taking off work early. "I love his love. But I am worried about my heart." Jane had a CD she just had burned so she could play in her car a chant. The religious male voices rang in high notes the Latin love of her God. She spoke out loud this time, "Yes, I do love him. God, you have directed me. His purity, my purity. His impurity, my impurity. The inside of his heart... Mine...!" It was like she was coming to grips with the immensity of love. And she was doing fine. Yes, Jane was serious about this love, not gleeful yet, but serious. This was a love that was tasting very fine to Jane.

The Colliding Atoms - Up, Down; Strange, And Charmed

*C*anadian geese, in their usual Vs, were heading up north. Since the climate changes of the new millennium, many of the birds stay in Ohio all winter, splashing in local ponds and lakes. Most homeowners did not like this. Their fecal matter made huge piles of smelly filth on golf courses, parks, lawns, and streets. The geese came in twos. Some scientists point out that the geese mate for life. Their rich musical honking must communicate their deep feelings to one another. Jim was watching them now. His new love was catching onto their love. Now, he was understanding their sounds. Viewing the depths of their desires for one another. And knowing they had inadequacies also, but knowing they had qualities that made them beautiful.

In the past, each day Jane arrived home she would get her work done. Vacuum, wash dishes, make supper, or clean and press her clothes. Things had changed. Jane awoke early and did her duties. The evenings were saved for love. Like George Washington's rules of civility, Jane put away all matters of a hectic life to spend focused time with her lover. Jim did the same. And their love grew. Like all love should. A day at a time becoming larger and deeper, where at times a smile means more than thousands of romantic words. Jim and Jane's countenances became one. Their reality was not just in dreams now. A gentle sweep became their life.

Still, strange times came.

"It is the evening, and I feel things have changed between us." Jane says, "It is the evening, and I feel things have changed between us. I can repeat what you say, can't I?"

"Yes, you make me understand my concerns by doing that. Another woman?"

"Yes, another woman. There will always be another woman. But, will she love you?"

"I do not think so. I pray that that will never happen."

"Your prayers will be answered."

"I hope so."

"Jesus said you can hope. But never swear to God that what will happen will happen. Jesus said heaven is the throne of God. You cannot swear by the throne, cannot swear by the feet upon the earth, you cannot swear by any city because every city is the place of God, cannot swear by even your own head because you head has the hairs of the divinity. All are owned by the One. Still, you can hope."

"I love you."

"I love you. It is worthwhile to love. To love you."

"We colliding atoms are the charms of God."

At these words, the two each night would see each other as bits of jewels touched by immortality. The relaxing charms of God. Up, down, the atoms swim in the vast sea of space. These odd pieces of his creation seem to be charm, opposed to the desolate magnitude of the rest of the cosmos that seems to just float for no reason.

Each night, the two were together. They looked out the window. In the darkness, they saw poems of light and definitions of evil. The chaos was there, but because they were in love, it did not bother them anymore. Chaos' questions had thousands of words. Jim and Jane did not ask if they were huddled in harmony. A pair does not ask that question if they have love. No doubts ever arise concerning that gift.

Sin is lying in the road waiting for a traveler that has not love and who is looking for God. If he knows it is sin, he knows there is a God. The man knows that the answer is a one-room house, a place to store himself until all answers come. The answers are gilded by tinges of golden love. The perfect harmony is love. The man asks, "Am I answer the harmony, or do I wish entanglements so that I can gaze on another in the distance? Do I want the distance?" Chaos has the questions that have all the words angry and alone. It does not hide but still is sought. One who comes into God's realm must learn that chaos, destiny, and harmony are all in letting God alone to do his work with you. The quiet, non-spoken poem is in God's breath, or shall we say breadth?

The math of it all is a primary algebra. A transposition, a reflex, a demonstration, a series of circles inside the square that are a life in Buckeye, in Cleveland, in America, in the world, a dot in the cosmos, the meaningless of time.

Jim and Jane repeated the word love. The demonstrations of the word love. Subsequent demonstrations, and they traveled into the key indices of the procedures that surround effortless love. Detailed accounts happened. Spaces and voids dropped in so that they could see the importance of love. Like they truly needed time to see the gift from afar. Occultation's, iterations, extensions, integration's, generations, echelons, modified transpositions, cross transitions, and multiple consequences of the act of love needed to be followed, spoken, and accomplished in the infinite time that was proceeding. Jane and Jim's equations were old yet new to the cosmos. Many journeys need to be pushed upon them. And they were by a God with a timeless heart.

Infinite Density

*L*ove and the end of one's time and the beginning of another's time became a one that was indefinable. Two were in a mood to give totally a big energy of themselves to each other. The azure color of emotion, love the calmer of where death will eventually take them. Jim and Jane. The two talk of wedding, seeing a pastor, the ceremony, and having a child late in life. The dense weight as the softness of being in love surrounds the two. The two as one. "Love, I do love you, cannot believe it, still, I do love every part of you." Jim speaks, retells the phrases, speaks of them again and again, over and over, and it never gets boring to his lady. Jane smiles. "All of that. All that you say. I do. I am willing to say the words now. I love you. Always. Be mine. Mine. Until the end of our time. And I am yours. Yes, I mean that. I have felt that. That our love will grow. That it will never end. That God has told us we are meant to be one. That we were one in the past and that love is eternal, and the oneness is now. We are now. Ever we will be. And that is truth. Love, the only word to live by." Jim smiles through this jaunt. Holding her hand. Touching Jane with the 'evers' of a God that has decided to shine upon them.

Looking into her deep blue eyes. Knowing this is the ultimate gift he has given them.

"Azurine, your eyes. Beauty. I love you, every part of you. You are fine for me. I wish you the best. I think only of you. And this phrase will be my ever. You, alone. Never even the thought of another. We as one." Jim looks down. His lady knows his feelings. She looks down. Jane feels the same humility. Like they both know that the ultimate gift has somehow been given to them. This gift has made them feel warm inside, has made them feel good, made the two feel that no gift they have ever been given to close to this one. This one.

"The intensity. Yet, the light aromas of spring flowers every season as we transpose our singularity into our duo. I love you, my Jim. Your eyes are in a quaint array because of your light. You see me and see my love. It is like I do not have to say the word anymore. But I will say the word, over and over."

"The peculiar sounds of your stringed instrument play for me. The sound inspires me. Your voice. Please keep speaking to me. The evening, after work, will be our time to play our songs to each other."

"Yes, Jim. Yes. My mental condition is for you. You are my learned one. Moreover, I am built up by you. Your equivocal hints of oneness. Love. There is singular feature of the future with you and I being so together that we think and do alike.

Yet are two. Why did God strike us? I do not know. I do not wish to know why. I thank him for us."

"Jane, may I say I love you too much. I do not feel I can. I am enchained by love's superstitions. We are the impressions of love's regards. I dwell in the tenanted, and they do not have it. You with me. You. I keep talking and feeling your vibrations coming into me. I love you."

"God, his influence, strikes me every moment of the times we have together. His influence, his force, conveyed to us in terms of touching and looking into one another's eyes. Together, our kindness possesses no shadows."

"Jane, thank you, thank you for allowing me to see God and you and one. God's family mansion looms. It is positive. The peculiarities. The form and substance of the home. The one child, all coming to us now. We are seeing all of this. We will be married. The pastor will have sweet words. God's spirit will be with us that moment as it is now."

"The effect of our married walls will present a whiteness to our united being. Our child will understand. He understands now, how he is thought of. We will venture knowing death will come and will never be afraid of death; its torments will never touch us again. Our son will know all these things and feel the freedom and roam over life's terraces, and his journey, too, will be endless."

"The gray walls will turn white. Our castle will be humble. Yet, it will have the warmth that is needed to live well. The morale of our existence will enter our child. He will see it all. A lot of empty talk will never be necessary."

'Slaves, gentle slaves we will be, and our anomalous species of will has found the weight of God and are happy about it all."

"I shall perish, knowing that the word means little. And so will you. And our son will see the folly of life and smile about it all. The dreams of a pastoral God are endless. They will never be lost within us."

"I will not dread the errors in our future. I know God has his way. And that way will be all good. The results, we will relish them, even if at first we have doubts."

"I shudder when I feel that the most foolish incident may swell in our lives to mean more. These agitation's, as we look back, will mean little. Our souls will reign over them."

"I love the depth of you, every one of your words. They are all correct. They mean much to me. I will learn to have no abhorrence of danger. Danger's terror will never strike me down. I have you, and that is the gift I need to continue. And continue I will, with you. Isn't it funny, that argument we had before we met, I mean, in our dreams? It means nothing now. We have the power of our love."

"A love, a love. I could talk all night to you. I love you. I am unnerved, almost pitiable. But I love you. Sometimes I feel I must abandon the boredoms of life, the depths of reason, just to be with you. I love you. Ever. The grim fantasies of life do not hinder me anymore. I have you. I love you. I need not worry over these empty things anymore."

"Yes, you explain it well. No fear, no fear nevermore. I have you now. I regard you with astonishment. There is no mingling of dread for this one. I find it almost impossible that I have such feelings for you."

"Yes, and more. The sensations put me in a stupor, yet it is a lively one. I am expanded. My eyes follow your every sigh, all your energies. I retreat with your steps into a love that has no time. Immortal, that is what I feel for you."

"I admit that much of my peculiar love could be traced to a more natural and far more palpable origin. My parents had this kind of love. Your increase of amore leaves me the first of an ancient, glorious malady. Love."

"We will marry even though we have been wedded through eternity."

"I do. Our 'I do's' have been said. And we will continue to say them forever."

"Forever."

"Yes."

"Your last word is our first>"

"Yes."

"And it will continue."

"Yes."

"For all time."

"Yes!"

Again and again, this is Joe Taylor, CNN, and I have the latest, as far as this scary, I mean, possibly scary scene in El Paso, or at least, nearing El Paso, Texas. the eighteen-wheeler continues to roll. It has hit stop signs, nearly hit animals, and almost hit innocent bystanders, but it continues to roll at fast speeds. Bystanders are wondering if it will stop for gas, or diesel fuel. All are wondering what will happen as it nears the concentrated part of this big city in Texas. The horror! Who is this man? Why? Why did he take control of this monster vehicle, and why is he driving so fast? Questions, always questions. This is Joe Taylor of CNN and we will always be here, for you and for everyone, giving you the latest breaking news from the world. We will keep you informed. Thank you.

With the heft of all matters, is there a weight to carry? Jim and Jane sit and talk and look into one another's eyes and see clarity that is easy to carry. What they have on the TV cannot take from them. The calculus of love. All the complexities still do not distract from the benefits of touching it. Love: the marked state, the integral parts of love. The letter l is large and means that love is beyond any understandable math. The unmarked state of love and the unknown, and the known indicators create an easiness that no one questions. The consequential expressions of love bring the two into an equation that has not been found. Yes, even the large equation, $E = mc$ squared, means there is no meaning. This equation was thought up to define the strength of God. These simple letters and one number are the most inaccurate equation. But it means God's immensity, and his light. And all this is integrated and real. All of this is located in the pure hither. As the canons of love continue to show themselves as the future abounds. Yes, in all of us. In Jane and Jim.

The two know the darkness of their real past. But they speak to one another as one, in this day's daylight. You can hear their whispers as shouts on the rooftops. Love is. Yes. And so, time flows. The blind in love lead the blind. And if they walk into an occasional ditch, like Einstein did, so what? The dirt will not hinder them. Because they have love to clean their essences.

Black Holes Are Not Black

*H*ardy Woodcocks in Buckeye. Jane had never seen one there before in her years on Notre Dame. Yes, two came, a pair, with love in their hearts. The beauty, their warming sounds.

Jane, again and again, thought that love would fall. In her forty odd years of time, this was her experience speaking to her quiet self. The question was always when. Still, she knew this was going to be a different trip, a positive one that was about one subject: God/love, in that close, exact order. And in her heart time was not relevant. Just because her mind taunted her did not mean her mind was correct this time. Yes, the sequential side of her mind played games with her. Two follows one and three follows two and four follows three. Her heart told her that there was no four here. There would be Jim, Jane, and a child.

The Woodcocks' protective colors rendered them virtually invisible with the countryside. These two were easily seen by Jane. The birds zigzagged, the whistling of their delicate wings as they darted from branch to scrub each other on another branch. It was like they were in a flight of courtship. The male seemed to fly high, up to the elevation of the clouds in northeast Ohio, their spirals, then flat down to the dull earth, calling beautiful tweets as the female watched, head tilted upward to see her mate. Love was in the air, surrounding the couple. A smile came to Jane's face as all seemed in order.

The cerulean, evening sky of spring spoke to the two as they met at Jane's house on Notre Dame. The watchet blue magnified the intense love they felt for each other and their futures.

Hello again. This is CNN'S Joe Taylor speaking to you from El Paso, Texas. We will show you the replay in a minute, but something interesting just happened here with this eighteen-wheeler and the man who hijacked the truck. The vehicle was heading into downtown El Paso. It had slowed to normal speeds as our helicopter followed it. Without a signal, the truck stopped and the man who was driving it got out, got down on his knees, you know, for a few seconds, and then got back into the massive vehicle and put it in gear. There it is. Watch this. Rather odd, for a man, a bald-headed man, who is breaking the law, to stop breaking it for a few seconds, pray to his god, and then keep breaking the law, getting back into his vehicle and driving away. The event confused this reporter. Now, back to your regularly scheduled news programs here on CNN. This is Joe Taylor. Goodbye.

Jane and Jim had begun watching the taping of this news event. As they sat having a cup of tea, Jane asked Jim if he had caught any new glimpses of this news on his tape machine as he played back a bit every other day. Jim said, "No, I wait for you to come to my house. I wait for you to join in the humor of this poor man who was caught by a megabucks news company, who both should spend some time getting their priorities straightened out. Life has gotten a bit funny in our rich country, hasn't it?" Jane laughed, "Yes, but I do like to see the media brought to their knees. All of us get humbled in our lives. Even Mr. Turner and his monstrous dollars are laughed at. He knows that."

In unison the two said, "But let's talk about something else."

Love. The two talked of love, and more love, as they touched each other with soft hands and looked into one another's eyes. Learning every moment what gift had been given to them. Jim said, "Via amore. The ways of our love are breathless. I do love you, and I must say it and say it, in all the ways that I know."

"Yes, you must. And I must feel it. And I do."

Jim spoke over and over many words about love as Jane listened intensely, "We men love to love, seven nights a week. We have desires about love. Love does not endure by reason. No logic within; we must love, and when we find love and if the love holds, we feel as good as good about life and what it offers us. The heat of love brings us the security we silently wish for. The truths and faithfulness of life is magnified when love enters. It has for me. I love you."

"Yes."

"Our marriage will be only half the depth of love. The words, the cleric, our friends and relatives, and more words, and all will mean little compared to the gift God has decided to give to us. Our love will need these words. Still, they are only half of what love is. The other half is beyond any words. Love is deeper than words, beautiful as beauty. Times like these, it is difficult to get to the core, so we must just know it is there and relish in what time has given us."

"Yes, I love you Jim. These are the moments I want to hear your words. They mean much to me. I understand your fragile nature. Still, I draw from your strength of vision. You are mine. I am yours. I will look into your eyes and listen to you. Yes."

"Old Pythagoras had more to say than math. He said something like, 'Many words are engraved in tables and pillars, but those compacts that are made with wives are inserted in the children that come.' We will have one, and he will understand what the man said who invented the truths with triangles. And love."

"Yes."

"You will go through immense pain, and then you will forget. Having our little boy, John, will be a glorious gift."

"Yes."

"It is better to marry the one you love than to burn in the absence of love. Single life is a misery. I will be happy to deal with your inadequacies."

"Yes, I feel the same about you."

"My fire will constantly burn for you."

"Yes, and me too."

"You must know that I have been celibate for you. When the time is right, I will come to you, and we will then be the consummate union. Will you trust me on that day?"

"I do."

"I will raise myself, and be one with you and with God. And our constant smiles will brighten. This time will be glorious. As we welcome God's vision into our unified selves, and then a child will come and he will understand what we as two understand in his one, tiny body."

"And he will smile up at us."

"Our wedding, our conception of a son, our living will be a wedlock between the eternal soul and our souls."

"Yes."

"I will love you kindly most of the time. There will be times you doubt me. Still, that will be the workings of a good marriage."

"There will be much planning about our marriage. Dear, there will be much stuff for you to endure. You will endure. The day will come this fall, a beautiful, blue time of year when the sky reflects the warm colors of the leaves, but the coolness of this time of year will not injure our love. We will go on and on. Our love."

"Jane, you are beautiful."

"Yes, and you too."

"In Romeo and Juliet, Shakespeare wrote, 'Did my heart love until now? I forswear it, the sight! For I never saw true beauty until this night.' Each night, it is an increase for me, as well for you, because we will look into one another's eyes. We will see the peace we have been searching for our whole long lives. The peace is here, yes. Peace is here."

"Yes."

"Einstein and his black holes did not know that love makes them the depths of light. That God hides love until he is ready to give it. Many see black. We see quiet light. And eternity."

"Yes."

"One hour of love with you is beyond anything Einstein ever said in his totality. My gratitude is for your love. Please be patient with me. I will transmute all my life into a love, a strong love for you. You will see."

"Yes."

"You, as you age, will feel such a fire in your heart for me that it will warm you in the coldest of winters. On bad days, it will dry the deepest tears you have in your eyes. Your will will be warmed by my sighs. You will know me as well as yourself."

"Yes."

"The sun will swallow us up because it will love our heat. We will understand it then. We will be dreamers of a new world. Such our pure love."

"Yes, yes."

"We will say our vows. Yet, this tiny moment we are one, as water with wine, will be a wonderful gloss. Your torment will be one with mine. Your delight will be one with mine. Your singing will be one with mine. I will hug you as I do now and we will be one, and I will kiss your forehead as I do now. And I will touch your tender wrists as I do now. All will have a fineness of being with us. We will hang together so softly."

As Jane looked up into Jim's eyes, she said, "Yes."

"Arguments will be less. They will be a diversion. And that will be their only purpose."

"Yes."

"I am your joy. You are mine."

"Yes."

"We will, as we are doing now, hug forever. Even as we proceed through our days without each other, we will be hugging each other. That will be our love. A fine definition."

"Yes."

The embracing, the touching, the being one in front of a God who knew all and was all, meant much to ones who knew the tough sides of life, who experienced the rigors. All was forgotten when they looked into each other's eyes and saw the girding future.

"I see you with loving eyes. I feel you with loving hands. I hear you with loving ears. Our love voices ring with songs for each of us. Our loving souls combine. Our loving bodies cling each to each in a mindless sweep of eternal time. I love you. You me."

"Yes."

"You favor me and draw me near. Your intimate 'yeses' draw me closer to you. Face to face, I see much of you. I feel much of you. Our love. The love will draw great life from us as we bond into the ethereal."

"Yes."

"The workings of our wills are from above. The close workings are curious. And when love is its center, goodness comes. The embraces. The love. The beauty. The love. The wrestling of the tempests in our lives will ultimately mean nothing. The love. The cheerful courage we will show to all. The love. The clouds. The love. The eyes. The love."

"Yes."

"Like as us virgins, our wedding night will be one. Until we experience, all our talk will not add up to a second of that night. It will be like we are both clothed in brocade. How can we explain this?"

"Only by doing. Even our words after the sweep of this gift will mean little."

"One cannot explain conjugal happiness to one who do not possess it. And to add to this love, a child will be created in the instant that is our bliss."

"I will be full grown. I will be near my lover's side. It will be the true, glorious experience. I will be more fervent in my devotion to you."

"Yes."

"Your jewels will be your thighs."

"Yes."

"Your breasts, the little baby."

"Yes."

"Your neck will be ivory."

"Yes."

"Your emotions will add up in your heart."

"Yes."

"Your head and the skin will be as soft as toffee."

"Yes."

"Your desire, an eternal gift to me. And I will love you as fully as you love me. What a wonderful gift."

"Yes, thank you."

"We will be in the entire sensory realm that night."

"We are now."

"Glory to you. I love you. Our secret will be our love. Our union. One man, one woman."

"And we will not truly comprehend any of this. We will do. And that will be fine. Our love will continue to blossom. In winters as in summers."

"I say, 'Ah Gautama, our sacrificial fires will never burn out, not even smolder.'"

"My dear woman, you are mine, ever. Yes!"

"Yes."

"Your vulva, my coals, your sparks, my flame, your slowness, my understanding, your sacrifice, my acceptance."

"The semen. Then him. From this oblation arises a son. The beauty of love, of God!"

"You are so beyond my thoughts. Thank you my dear."

"Yes."

"The sun and the moon will be joined, and time will stop as we go on and on."

"Yes."

"The red and the black of us will be joined in an ultimate blue. Beauty will then come to us the rest of our lives."

"Yes."

"Our bodies will be colored by the quicksilver of life. The body of your future will become his, the little boy. My will becomes yours as I protect you both with my wonder."

"Yes."

"My tingeing seed will enter."

"Yes."

"I will become your words."

"Yes. And I will know what you do not know. And you will have a peace because of this. And you will know my untruths. All reside in the infinitely small seed."

"My love, I love your womanly soul. Lay all your acts on my heart. God, who sees all, brings all to light, and knows me as a dissolute man and you as powerful woman."

"Yes."

"We will never have any carnal connections. Our sex will be a synonym with love."

"Yes."

"We will realize God each moment of each of our days."

"Yes."

"And exalt in his glory."

"Yes."

"And many times, will our love bite our lives?"

"I do not know. Still I love you, yes."

"Dear, our souls have many veils. And we will leave them be. We will not discuss any of them. For the soul should never be revealed, unless we wish to speak to God."

"Yes."

"Love is our subject of thoughts."

"Yes."

"We will profit from our love. We need not money. Having selves will be our wealth."

"Yes."

"Honey is the sweet juice of the flowers. Our love is their tradition. The closest staple to the intent of love."

"Yes."

"I must begin to leave you tonight. But you will go with me. We have discussed unheard of things about love. And I feel good, almost as good as Jesus did when he spoke his glorious words to the common people."

"Yes, you are my savior on this earth."

"Yes, and I love you, and will say these three words forever to you. You will hear them even in heaven."

"Yes."

"We are joined unto the Lord."

"Yes, we will say our vows although they have already been said."

"Thank you."

"Yes."

"The solar self of love has come to us."

"Yes."

"Tonight, the closer our embrace, the sweeter our kiss." Jim joined with Jane and did not speak another word. They looked into one another's eyes and saw that time was still. They went to their beds. They had a pleasant sleep filled with embraces. Their love kept going on and on into the night. It was a good night that was full of stars. And warmth. And love.

Ones Never Escape
From A Black Hole

*T*oday, Jim and Jane only needed to situate reality, and all its mechanisms, with love. Maybe the two took a while finding it because their expectations were high. They believed love existed prior to knowledge. Compared to what love becomes once it gets encompassed with the framework of necessities and possibilities it is constructed by the subjects without being modified and its intrinsic genres, which remain independent, become real. At first glance, reality may appear completely absorbed or consumed at its two ends by love, but then it proceeds. Love is reduced to nothing more than a particular case a month other than possible other cases. But it always rears its emotions and becomes love again and takes over. If allowed to grow love becomes rich. Love becomes understood and promoted from the lower ranks of the observable to the higher ranks of interpreted reality. Still, a couple of old ambiguities needed to be cleared up.

For Jane and Jim, the first was to see a certain form of idealism in this subordination of reality and love. The lovers' cognitive tools need to be gazed at. Then, there are those that this remains completely false. Jane and Jim? Internalized operations come into the picture. This explains the surprising convergence of mathematics and physics and endearment.

The second ambiguity might result from the distinction of love between the object as it is and the objects interpreted by the lovers. Let's look at Kant and his distinction between love and the thing itself (the noumenon). And the thing as it is revealed (phenomenon). Seems though that all of this is false. And they do not explain love entirely. Every little progress seems to open new regresses for the scientist. This means that the absolute difference between love and the objects and subjects diminishes the functions of the successive approximations. There always remains a relative distance between all the words of love and love itself. Limits need to be put upon anything that comes to earth. Still, are we saying that there are limits to love? Most would disagree. Even the scientists. There are no limits to the unknowable and immutable noumenon of love.

What is to be learned from the above decrees? Nothing, most will say. Jim and Jane agree. Any necessity, such as love, remains conditional and will need to be transcended by an immense God. God will make any apodictic judgments that are necessary to love intrinsically expanding. Any scientist who is in love knows it is beyond any of his theories.

The cyanic dimensions of love, how its blueness transcends the dimensions of time and space surprises most people. Jim and Jane did not discuss every bit of information about love. But they felt them. Every scientific particle made their lives a blue that had a dull clairty, an opaqueness that they felt they could touch any time they wished. All the blue tones brought smiles to their faces, smiles that occurred at work, at play, at home, even as they slept, and even when they were apart.

On another day they awoke, showered, went to work, and met that night at each other's houses. Each morning, before they entered their cars and drove off, within their houses, they called each other and told each other where they were to meet. "I love you" and that phrase was discussed. The meeting place and love was always discussed. The two had quietly directed lives moving forward. To Jim and Jane love existed as the first extirpation or determination of a kind God. Both had met and taken in one of greater quality. In a unified, unspoken manner they both felt love could not exist in our world without God's intervention. They felt like stopping occasionally and watching this Other pass in front of them as they bowed. The air around them was full of God and his rituals. Both knew that other regular people thought them a bit crazy. But this was love. Nothing else mattered. Days went wildly by and everything was falling into place. Jim and Jane. Their love was blossoming in front of them, and they could view it, and that love inspired them to keep going on with smiles on their faces. The future and the experience differed only in that both thought it easy to dream, but putting the dream into a continuous movement was difficult. Reality was something to think about. It involved much work. Dreams only went on if one closed their eyes.

Cleveland, this godly city, races through Jim's mind as he works his way into work. He thought to himself in the car with the radio off, "I am because I know. These are my hours of hours and I will be within them with my Jane alongside. At forty-two

I am allowed to digress, to look back on my religious life. This city of God, this town, the buildings, the sweat are strong, and I must be like them. Yes, I am only the son of a working couple, but I know love for its gift. I have true love now. I am happy. Jane is beatific. I love God, I love myself, and I feel a deeper love for my Jane. My Jane.

It is like all glorious justice has turned to a perfect judgment for me. She is my perfect being. Jane is as tender a being who walks for me. When she touches my arm, I smile. When I touch her delicate skin, I smile. Such is life for me now. A wonder. Love is a final peace. We need God. And that is all we need. God gives to us things we are not even sure about until we try to be godly and look deep into them, then we see the magnitude, the holy magnitude of it all on this everlasting globe.

Years ago, as a baby, my mother took me and baptized me in Lake Erie. She quietly spoke the words, 'Father, Son, Holy Spirit, dwell with him and be with him forever, allow me to be his priest, and somehow show him the Trinity's love.' God, you did all for me. And to add to this you gave me love. I love you. I love you. I feel that is all I can ever say again that has any meaning to you and to Jane. You have made me understand loving Jane by loving you first. Wow!"

This is Joe Taylor again, CNN, and we have breaking news for you this morning. After four hours, this supposed tragedy has ended. The man who hijacked the eighteen-wheeler has given up and is in the custody of the El Paso police at this time. This is happening as this copter I am in following this huge vehicle around the area. Let's watch the replay. Time stood still as the truck stopped, a man got out, held up his hands, and the police took him into custody. Simple as that. No explanations. The El Paso situation has ended. You are seeing it here, and only here. There, there it is. Watch carefully as the police take the bald-headed man into custody, and this is over. No one hurt, no one killed. Everything is fine in the southern most part of these United States. Everyone is happy it is over. Insanity did not win out. No one hurt. Now, we turn you back to the breaking news at the desk at CNN. This is Joe Taylor. The El Paso hijacking is over. As we obtain the details and the why's of this crime, we will relay it to you on CNN. Have a good day, have a good life.

There were many things finished, and things just beginning.

Jane feels the ecstasy of love. The supreme estate of love has descended upon her, and her state of demonstration was extreme; her heart murmured for now she had purpose, and that purpose was being in love. The madness that was God came to her and it felt better than the sanity of human identity. There was a shattering and tearing of the veils over her life. The modalities of space and time did not mean much anymore. She had Jim. Discursive reasoning was in the ditch. The deep wisdom that the world feels means little to a God who understands that love is the best thing he bestows on two who become one. The supralogical is superior. The logical is the logical and means little to the tendencies of those in true love.

Jane thought, "We people do not understand the plunge of love until we take it. We have no understanding who drove us to this ultimate gift."

Her ride to work meant more this day and each succeeding day. For love made time still. The quiet seemed to be fine for Jane. Before, she drove to work with the radio blasting. Now she allowed the quiet of the hum of the car to invade her thoughts about Jim, her total thoughts of love. "I like the madness that has come over me. It is positive, all the way. I love my Jim, waiting every second for the evening when we can be one, touching each other with the security God gives us. Love. All is love. All."

"The usually quiet hagiography of our church will glow over us when we marry. The pastor will speak. The chorus will sing. We will look into one another's eyes and see the indescribable warmth of our beings brought together. We will be sanctified. Love is the impenetrable mask in which the wisdom of God is concealed and then brought to light as it descends into our faces. Jesus felt this when God penetrated him those last three years with his love. He had a glow. We will have a glow. An eternal one."

Jane knew Shakespeare must have known. The method to the madness that is love is never questioned because the prize is one all of us have truly been seeking. Love, love, more love. The words hit us deep in our heads, and most of us never let the thoughts of love out, but they are always there, deep within, waiting to throw themselves out, but still we feel we have to control them, the thoughts, but we should not. We should let love shout as loud as love gets in life. We should. Jane was feeling all this as she settled into work for another day.

We Are All Composed
Of Language

"*D*amn hard day, Hon!"

"Still, it is good to be with you, good to see your face and good to get a hug from you."

"Damn hard day. They lowered my pay. Said it was the economic problems in the industry. That maybe the future would open things up. You know, all that standard bureaucracy stuff. Tired of hearing it!"

"Yes, I know how to use it. Being a boss, you get non-emotional with your language. Sad, still, I love you. I love you whether you get a raise or a drop in pay, whether you have a good job, a bad job, or no job at all. I love you, my dear"

"I need your words. I need your hug. Your sweet kiss."

"Perhaps we were meant to love one another, to support one another. I know I am getting philosophic, but maybe we were born to love one another. Simply and genuinely, we are there for each other. Sweet Jim, we were never meant to experience the travesty of life with love."

"Yes."

"Your eyes are powder blue this evening. I love you. The sadness you are going through. It is sadness. It will be mine for a little while. I will kiss it away. So, you will have a smile on your face."

"Yes." Jim leaned over and kissed Jane's forehead. He said, "You carry me. Jane, you are carrying me across this minor gulf, keeping me from the deep water."

"Yes, love has taught us to look across that gulf. Love has taught us that it just does not include looking into one another's eyes but in looking outward together in the same direction. Love is the eyes."

"Yes."

"I want to talk about the pastor and how we honestly talked with him last night."

"Yes."

"All these years going to the same church, St. Rita's down here in Buckeye, and we never met. Never saw each other because we worshipped at different masses, and the priest says, 'Such is the way sometimes. I never understood love.'"

"Yet, he knows us well enough to give us his blessing. And he loves our plans for our wedding. The date, next June, a little over a year from now. He is secure with everything about us. He cannot believe; he said it sounds like we were meant for each other. That God must be smiling, smiling on us"

"He said God showered us with plenty of love later in our lives, and that love, whether for decades or a day, is the Lord's supreme gift to us. That we have invited him to our wedding, and all is well."

"Yet, don't you feel so free? We are becoming one. One! I feel I can walk outside and see beauty. Being with you is like being with a birth. It still is a gift. The last time I see you is the first time I see you. You are with me ever. All is glorious for us."

"Yes!"

"It abides for us, the unity. We will abide by its unity. And feel that being together is just fine, even if we never talk again to each other. Just seeing that you are around is fine for me, fine for you. Every day is a Sunday."

"Love is fine for itself. Fine as fine can ever be. I love you. I will never stop telling you."

"You looked into my eyes and asked for my gift. And I applauded. The vital principle of love is with us. I love you."

"And the chorus at our church will sing for us."

"We will have some tears within our eyes when we hear them. The same tears will be in our eyes as our priest asks us to say I do. And we will keep them in our eyes. Because they are tears of joy."

"We will love each other in one direction."

"The direction will be toward God."

"Thanksgiving will be every day for us. We will get on our knees before we hug, before we sleep."

"The instinctive movements of our personalities will know what is working for us. You will not love me because of my personality, my money, my future, or my principles. You will love me because of my being. I will love you because of yours. We will love because of our forevers and evers."

"Love only obeys itself."

"And we will obey love."

"Egotism protects us. But love humbles us. We have needed the balance, and the balance is here. Love."

"We recognize each other in each other."

"Oh, do you remember what our priest said. He loves us. Sees good things in us like how my older brother, the one who died at birth, is now me because I have found love in you. I was touched by his words. And how he said you are showing the depth of your father, how his quiet attitude made him beautiful."

"Yes."

"And how we as two were made to be one because the Lord had congealed in his wealth and had given it all to us."

"Yes. Please let me kiss you now. Now." And they did. And the bliss was the peace that they had always wished for, had always known would happen, and felt the quality that they knew would be indescribable.

"Our kiss will never be over. It will last and last. Forever, as for this brief moment in a long day."

"How we will never bore each other with it. I am sure we will bore others. But never ourselves."

"Love."

"Sweet, everlasting love."

"Yes."

"We are all the glorious words of love."

"Yes, and we are one as we speak."

"The Father knew that."

"Yes, he did."

"And it made his day."

"And it made our lives."

Ultimate Time Lies
Within Ultimate Time

S ome things do not happen often here. The morning sky is cloudless and dyed an ultramarine this Sunday.

Jane and Jim made plans to attend the morning mass at church this glorious day. Father was there with his Christian smile and hardy handshake. The hour service was sweet. On the walk to the car, Jim started in with his love talk, "Love has divined and wound tight into our talents. They have been dormant these years before our love met each other. I will help my neighbors more than I have been. You will make your work at the office even sharper. And we, who love life, will cherish it even more than in the past."

"Yes." Jane's smile always shone on these positives.

"I love you on this bright day. Do you feel the warmth of spring in the air? Our downtrodden Buckeye seems cleaner and friendlier today." The whispering in and around the church continued. It sounded like a precious hum in the breeze.

"Yes. I felt our son today. He feels nearer. I am starting to feel his love coming. He will be a strong boy, just like baby Jesus, and he will understand the ways of God just like our Savior."

"Yes."

"We have become good people. Our child will follow us. We will need not much talk to get him there. He will watch how we lead our lives."

"I am a lover who has found his lover."

"Our love will make our son understand the mysteries of the divinity."

"We will love and like each other. And he will follow and find love on his own after we have passed. Our smiles towards ourselves will make him feel whole as a baby, as a child, and as a young adult."

"I know we will pass. It will be a sweet passing. And he will understand it all because we will teach him."

"Our created love will be fragrant to our son. He will honor us our time together. There will be a smile on his face."

"All will be in tune."

"Yes."

"Our sounds will be his. His ours. The rest will be the humble jumble of earth's life. Still, we will cherish it and celebrate it. Our son will not grow to be a Doubting Thomas."

"Yes."

"Love is the way love is."

"And our priest is amiable to us. He understands us. Does not question our intents. When we say goodbye to him today, we will hug him. He needs the love he espouses."

"Yes."

"Love brings our journey nearer to the knowledge of God."

"We celebrate that."

"Yes."

"We are preserving ourselves from the movements of death. Our prayers are one with the intent of God."

"Our love will not have shadows."

A male, winter cardinal, contrasted from the white of the constant dirty snow in Buckeye, was showing the lively sportiness of spring, the energy of new life coming. Repairing the nest, feeling the warmth of the afternoons in the neighborhood, he was sprucing his wings. The puddles from the cars on the streets were clearing. The water for the cardinals was getting tastier. Jim was feeling a deep knowledge that when you meet those of greater quality than yourself, you stop. You gaze and take in. And if she looks at you, you ask her for marriage. This was already done, and Jane accepted without a word. A lasting smile brightened the man's day. Certain vital moments in life do not need much conversation. The buildup to those moments does.

The generative process can be extended into a huge space that most may think is shallow but is not. Such a marriage is within the eyes of two lovers. From any expression, an equivalent one can come if you wait for it to come, if you are patient. Variables become non-sequiturs in a cosmos that derives its thrills in the intensity of human life. God is not disappointed because he does not view the evening news. To him, most of the news is good as compared to our anchors who have the truth switched around. There are two appearances that have variability. God and Channel 3.

Would be nice to unite the two orders. Still, many know that God's plans have little to do with us and our planned chaos. God does not value headlines. He does not speak in words anymore.

The Properties Of The Universe

"*I* 'm in a good mood this evening. It has been a rainy, spring day. The croci are blooming. The smell of an enduring life is in the air. Words are meaning less to me. Love is meaning more. I feel good about being here with you. I am more alive than ever.

Thanks for letting me talk.

At work, the men of business are becoming less important to me. Their short discourses are chats that have more to do with job justification than making the company bring in more money. The economy has much to do with that. And they have little to do with that. Yes, they feel good chatting, but it means little. But I will be good, stay within the work ethic, and keep bringing in my salary. Paying the bills is fine with me.

Thanks for letting me talk. I need to talk.

Ah, the leaves are coming to our trees. Living in Buckeye is getting to be worthy to me. Happy. The once dirty streets of winter are freshening. I feel alive. I feel worthy of our love. I love you. I know I haven't said that in a while, but know I feel it, all over myself and inside my soul. I feel your love and ours being one. Our wedding day will come and go, and our love will continue to increase because time will add to its depth.

I love you.

The atmospheric blue of life has penetrated me with your love. Calmed me. Yet, it energizes me with your spirit, your drive to love me more. And I love you more. Our blues are royal. Our personages are now one with a mellow power.

I love you.

I have found out that the big huge of the universe is love. I thought it was that empty infinity of space that was in my past. Now, I know it is full of your love and mine, and I bow to it, to us. Thank you for being alive. Still, I get the message that our love will continue. That God has given us the word forever, and now I understand it to mean that our togetherness is extremely esoteric and real and will last and last.

It's funny, I have been watching that silly video that got stuck on the recorder, you know, bit by small bit, watching it and seeing that it is a story of nothing, and it was meant to be. I only wish newscasters realized that they only thought it was meant to be headline news. But those nasty men and women only put on stuff that is nasty. Nasty comes from nasty, and it continues, and that is why the public gets bored with them and their evil displays. The man stole the truck and went a long way with it and did not hurt anyone, and all will be fine in the world. The tiny wrongs we do most of the time mean nothing, and that should be reported so that those in life should not feel bad about wrongs or try to do things that are really terrible just so they can beat the evil doers with something that is worse. Oh, I shouldn't even talk about such stuff. I should entirely love you.

Oh, my love! We are ready for marriage. We have talked to the pastor. The invitations are out. All the good stuff. Yet, I know we are already married, deep in love, and a child is coming, and he will be healthy and live a long time, and we will die nearly on the same day, and we will be each with each in eternity, and life will go on and on over this vast planet, and good things will happen in our good country, and your eyes will always touch me, and the depths of our stories will never be known, but that will not matter, because we have the ultimate gift from God and that is good enough, and time will space us by, and the meaning of the universe will never be known by any of us, even those of us who continue to investigate it, and all will be fine in our massive world, because we feel love, and that is good enough. Love is the colossal power of perfect beauty.

I love you.

All kinds of thoughts are in my mind. You love them. You accept them. I love you because your love agrees with my love.

I love you.

We need not worry about our lives, what we eat, what we have to wear. We look at the cardinals, the robins, the loons, the geese, the sparrows, the wrens, all the other birds we know nothing about, and we see the wind flashing past their wings and know that it is love. Love is their breeze. The birds neither plant or reap, neither store nor hoard, and God gives them enough food to live and continue to fly until he is ready to take them.

With us humans, the only difference is that we have some inner control. When we have made our peace with God, we choose to go, and God takes us. In a millionth of a second, his words hit our words and we know, when we are ready we will have his peace and leave, and all will be fine, and time will stop like it has in sections of our cosmos, and we will fly to those places and see a light that is beyond words. We are fine, and we will feel.

I love you.

I love being with you. You, my lover who lets me talk. Thank you. Ah, that is good, you gave me a kiss, a warm kiss, as we entwine our arms and show our love. I love you.

You let me talk. I love you.

The math of my talk is one about two. Our love, our properties will be one. All will be common and will indicate a need to be indicated. Our consequences will be acceptable because we decided on the rules. And our life will follow the rules. The content of the primary arithmetic has simple consequences in their demonstrations. Some will think the addends will be boring and tedious. But we know our theorems are true and beautiful. Images, examples, and proofs have become imaginary like x squared plus one equals zero. Imaginary and real in the flash of a moment. That is our love for each other. Yes, we will need time that we will need reuniting. We will be diving off into other arenas, but we will always find ourselves again, and we will lock ourselves in our equations and find out that they will both be coming out with the same answers. Math is equal and about love. We talk about each session as it comes. And fall, winter, summer, and spring will make us love each other more and more. The numbers in love will increase, as its beauty does.

I love you like a poem loves its words. Hills will rise across the valley. The Cuyahoga will clean up. Buckeye will explode again with much life. You and I will awake. We will spend our mornings together for a week. We will burn and not sweat. We will lie alone. At our kitchen table, Kafka will sip sentences, telling his short stories inside our heads, and we will smile knowing all this is happening and is as real as real. You and I will turn our heads towards the large window in our bedroom and hear our discs grinding like stones. The hills far off in other counties will feel like blending as all the heat of life wavers, and we will feel the blank weather of summer on our lives. We will dally with each other. A child will be born and as alive as ever, and all this will make us smile. I will say that the hills way off look like the greening of a good world, a satisfying world, and a world that will become one for thousands of years until the end of time. Our sightscreens will become larger as we, as a couple, will see the wholeness of the past and the future. We will not feel the surprises of death like those who live feel them. Death will taste like fresh apple juice. And be fine for us. Our hearts will jerk and feel the harmony of nature and time. We will feel our lives were short sentences and fine for their uniqueness. Fears and palpitations will leave us as God takes us to a place that was made of a thousand passive Edens. All will be finally well.

And I will say I love you. And you will imitate the beauty of our vastness. And splendor will reign.

Where love rules, there will be no will towards power. Such is heaven.

No shadows will be. I love you.

And the only tragedy in life is when folks forget about love. Do other things. And think they are important.

It is bad that many believe that love is the wind in trees and is gone the next day. True, it is wind, but it is one that lasts if you wish to feel it. Many feel it is a silly word. But it is a word, the best word, the one word that means more than infinity or God or the pulse of wooden lives. We must take time to stop our lives and say those words.

I love you.

A little more my lover. A few more words. Please. Thank you for allowing me this night with you. To let my words flow and just see you smile.

Love does not recognize the difference between peasant and pearl. The poor and the proud. The pheasant and the dried plum. Peace and peculiarity. Pomp and pestilence. We two love love.

Over forty years we waited for love. Love came. There was no need to worry. We have found the great gift; we glorify it and go on and on.

Yes, we have lost our common sense. Still, love provides our warmth. Yes, we have lost money. Still, love gives us the essentials and more. We have lost all meaning. Still, love gives us meaning beyond the boredoms of the real world. Love. Thank you – Love.

Love is loving you more than others. But still loving all totally.

Love in this is the promised land.

We are responsible for each. We are responsible for none other than our selves now. And as he comes, the little one, our responsibilities will be towards him. But first they will be for us. He will know we love each other.

Love, a simple man and a simple woman. The complexities will mean nothing because we love each other.

Love. We love each other, and we love the promise of what is to come."

Jane and Jim smiled at one another and broke off their time with one another and went to their homes and fell asleep and woke up and went to work and met again that evening so love could be felt more.

Children come down the aisle and face God, standing on the left side. They come down the aisle and stand on right side, facing rear of the church. The groom and pastor enter, come down the aisle, and stand in the center, facing the rear. Others flow. The bride enters with her father. He sits down after they reach the front. The wedding party assembles, facing front. The pastor moves up on platform. He speaks, "As we share in this wedding ceremony, it is well that we remember that, in the beginning, when God created the heavens and the earth, He concluded, "It is not good for man to be alone." So, He created woman to share in man's life - to assist in man's striving, to satisfy man's need. He also created the woman to be loved, honored, and appreciated by man. This is marriage, and it is for the purpose of joining Jim and Jane in marriage that we have come together today. The marriage of a man and a woman is viewed by God as an occasion of great joy since it marks the beginning of a relationship that is second only to our personal relationship with the Lord himself. But it is only through God that marriage becomes what he intends it to be. Let us acknowledge his place in this ceremony and see his blessing on this union."

The pastor then says, "Who presents Jane to be joined in marriage to John?" The father says the big "I do." Then, the reverend says, "The essence of any marriage relationship is love. Much of what we call love is a self-centered response, which will never form an adequate foundation for marriage. Love, by its very nature, is active and giving, not self-oriented and self-serving. Jesus Christ is the true example of love, and he has commanded us to love each other as he loves us. And how does he love us? First, he gives all for our sake, without hesitation or concern for himself. In other words, love puts the needs of the one loved ahead of the needs and desires of the lover. Next, from Jesus' example, we see that love shares all. There are no secret compartments, no hidden rooms, no locked closets in a successful love relationship. There is only openness and, as a result, trust, when husband and wife truly love each other. Finally, the Lord Jesus teaches us that love provides all. It provides security; it seeks to develop ability, and it shares the common purpose of obtaining what is best for the one loved. This kind of love is not impossible, but it is supernatural. Only God can love this way, and we can only love this way if we submit to him and depend on his Spirit to love through us. Therefore, as marriage partners, you must continually allow Christ to exercise his passion in your lives because he, and his dwelling spirit, will enable you to be a proper husband and good wife. Earlier, I said that the essence of any marriage relationship is love, but when we understand what love really is, we must recognize that the essence of any marriage relationship is our spiritual relationship with the Lord Jesus Christ, because without him there is no real love. The Apostle Paul gives us an additional description of love in God's words: 'This love of which I speak is slow to lose patience; it looks for a way of being constructive. It is not possessive; it is neither anxious to impress, nor does it cherish inflated ideas of its own importance. Love has good manners and does not pursue selfish advantage. It is not touchy. It does not keep account of evil or gloat over the wickedness of other people. On the contrary, it is glad about all men when truth prevails. Love knows no limit to its endurance; no end to its hope. It can outlast anything. It is, in fact, the only thing that still stands when all else has fallen.'"

Then the pastor says to the bride, "We must also realize that marriage is designed to be a picture of Christ and His relationship with those who believe in Him. In this picture, you, Jane, as you give yourself in submission and dependence to Jim, portray the role of the Christian who also gives himself in submission and dependence to Christ." He continues, "On the other hand Jim, as you love and keep Jane, you portray the love of the Lord Jesus as he expressed it toward the Christian. In view of this picture, there are specific instructions to both husbands and wives." The pastor turns and speaks to the bride, "To the wife, God says, 'Wives, be subject to your own husbands as to the Lord, for the husband is the head of the wife as Christ is the head of the church.' Jane, this is the command of God in his words and is designed to make your marriage relationship a thing of beauty and joy. So, in acceptance of this principle of God's words, do you now commit yourself to Jim, to be his wife, to join your lives together in living, permanent union as Christ is to the church?"

Jane whispers, "I do."

The pastor speaks to the bride. "Then repeat after me: I commit myself to you Jim, before God, to be your faithful and loving wife for all the years of our earthly life, to cherish our relationship in Christ and God's order for the family."

Now, the pastor speaks to the groom, "Jim, the command of God to husbands is, 'Husbands, love your wives as Christ loved the church and gave His own life for it.' Loving as Christ loved is the key to the enjoyment of all that God designed marriage to be. Without love the fullness you seek will turn into emptiness, the satisfaction into dissatisfaction. Therefore, do you willingly express your desire and intent to fulfill God's command to husbands, counting on the enabling ministry of the Spirit of God, and do you now commit yourself to Jane to be her husband?"

"I do."

The pastor to the groom, "Then repeat after me: I do commit myself to you, Jane, before God, to be your faithful and loving husband for all the years of our earthly life, to seek to love you even as Christ loves the church which is His bride."

"As you exchange rings let them be to each of you a constant reminder of these commitments you have made. Please repeat these words after me: I give you this ring, Jim, as a symbol of my love, and with it pledge my loyalty and devotion as long as we both shall live. And Jim, please repeat these words after me: I give you this ring, Jane, as a symbol of my love, and with it pledge my loyalty and devotion as long as we both shall live."

The exchange of the simple kiss. The two looked at each other and whispered in unison, "We will be with each other forever."

Then the two's tough thoughts about marriage start to creep in.

"We don't have enough money for a large reception. Well, we could afford a big party, but we'd be out of cash for hard liquor, wine, and party supplies. It's not really an option to go for a smaller gathering. We have to feed the whole of the people we know and those our parents know. It took a bit of humble apologizing to prevent the whole extended community from being invited. It's never easy to convince people that we're not rich enough to feed a thousand guests, especially with a camera in our hands. In the tradition of the bride and groom hosting a feast for the extended family and friends of the whole community. If all those people invited all their relations, we'd have a thousand guests here. As it is, there will be two hundred or so.

We need to go to a bank. The nearest bank is in Cleveland, and the journey takes forty minutes there and back. When we return, our hosts have made an entrance of love and will accept any get together we arrange and can afford. They love us as much as we love ourselves.

Our relatives tell us that the groom should bring good fortune to the marriage. We use the excuse of being good lovers to shirk our duty, and we ask all, plead to all, to do it for us. The truth is we just can't do everything. It was difficult enough to weigh our finances, balancing them on an ancient scale, wrapped in good health. We hear our money squeal as we get dressed and try hard to ignore it.

I can see it now. Jim gets the attention of the guests, and even some of the kids quiet down for a second or two. We sit expectantly and then grin as he starts saying a blessing for us while waving a white veil. Everyone is laughing because he's not sure what to say. We're the first people he's married. The blessing was traditionally given by an elder or by the priest of the wedding itself. Our ceremony is expanded a little. We move right to the next step. We have to get a good sign to tell us that the celebrations can begin. Jim's father and mother bring out a small silver case and place it in front of us. At this point we've moved onto a love seat set in front of a woven backdrop, and we look down at the case at our feet. Jim and his father and mother push the case back and forth, each unwilling to be responsible for the omen. Eventually Jim's mother opens the case and brings out love as a magical symbol about the size of a small apple. She pauses nervously before tossing it into the air. It's a mixed blessing. This means we can continue.

Everyone is in great spirits now and feels a massive energy of goodness, and the band starts playing. This chaotic singing gives everything a carnival-like feel. We are told that we must offer a drink to each guest and we make a round for everyone present. Everyone shares a drink. If a guest wants to pass on the strong shot, they touch the glass and then their mouth to show respect, and politely decline.

Everyone has had their ceremonial drinks. First, Jim's father straps on a watch and tells them it is time to party. As the groom, Jim is expected to follow with his own watch. Jane does her best, and the shrieks of laughter start up again. Sometimes, honesty can be cruel. Making a spectacle of yourself is a great way to make friends, and she is making dozens of friends. Jane is shown the woman's dance and does her best to perform. She pulls it off much more gracefully than Jim did and gets a big round of applause. After this, Jim gets a dance lesson from one of the bolder young boys. He wonders where he learned the dance.

After a while, Jim's father gets his energy flowing and begins to dance. This dance seems a little more serious, and he circles the crowd. He makes a swift cut to remove it from the crowd. He continues in a wisp to dance. He repeats this a few times and then passes life onto Jim. As Jim dances, he imagines good fortune. He prefers it to the peanuts that may come. How could any man not want fortune? Yet, Jim knows he has a different kind of wealth. This dance is the last formal step in the ceremony, and the rest of the night all play and dance to the songs and drink wine until each family closes their door in the hall and goes to sleep.

Time, A Property?
No, An Arrow

 prayer.

May on this day there be peace within...

May we trust our highest power that we are exactly where we are meant to be...

May we never forget the infinite possibilities that are born of faith...

May we use those gifts that we have received, and pass on the love that has been given to us...

May we be content knowing we are children of God...

Let this presence settle into our bones, and allow our souls the freedom to sing, to dance, and to bask in the sun...

For God is there for each and every one of us...

Let us show the love we have for each other by loving God in the same way...

A small prayer. Spoken without speaking it aloud. Caressed within our hearts. Always within the hearts of two who have become one.

The priest laughed and let things go on because love was there. Then, the speaking began as love needs to be discussed by two who are one. Speaking goes on because all those who were involved have touched love with their hearts one time or another in their lives. Traditional words were spoken because of the need. I dos. And leaves were naturally added by God to the trees surrounding the church, and spring became as gentle a season as it is at times when the cardinals, wrens, and the robins sing divine songs, and love became as docile as fingers touching can be and everyone at the church focused on the altar and three, the man, the woman, and God, as all the complexities of living simplified in front of the attentive audience, and fresh air came into the front doors, rice thrown later set itself on the sidewalks, smiles all over faces warmed the air, a hardy reception made be talk and talk, and later that evening, a voice said, a singular voice spoke, as each voice has its turn, and the other voices listened looking into eyes, the blooming of a huge love that controlled lives and the time remaining, "I love you."

Being spoken again, over and over, "I love you." As if it needed to ever be spoken, "I love you." Everyone there knew this. Of course, the next day people forget. People need a constant reminder that the word needs to be spoken a lot.

"That was beautiful dear."

"We are one, as we are meant to be, and the ceremony totaled love. I love you."

"Time spoke to us. I love you."

"All there were speaking to us in their best voices, their quiet voices. Silence."

"Arrows shot at us. Love."

"God counted us, each of us, and saw that we were pointed toward our ultimate love. I love you."

"God counts the hairs on our head. Know all things. Wishes to give us as a gift trust. He knows our love will last because he is the huge donor of love and knows we trust him."

"The math is totaled. The numbers have been in place. The uniting of two orders has become a quiet gift and needed to be said without re-numeration. The proof is the simultaneous demonstration of all the simplifications of all expressions. Our consequences will be the proof of love. No longer have we anything to justify in arithmetic because we have become love. Our complex algebra of love has been simplified by one equation, one plus one equals one. The demonstrable consequence is love. We float in numbers and become them as words are not enough to explain our destination."

"I love you."

"I wish you to be one always."

"I love you."

"I need to speak to you."

"This is about love."

"You are listening, your eyes are upon me. I love you."

"Our union, before time, now, on time, after, forever, beyond time is meant to be harmonious. Sure, life will have some downturns for us, but our love will be untied and united."

"Love is my gift to you, for you and I."

"You are earth and sky and warmth to me. I will feel like a peasant to you, taking potatoes out of the ground, and feeling like each one is a seed of your love for me."

"I love you."

"Sometimes, I know I will feel I am not giving enough to you. Then, I will see your eyes are accepting of me wherever I have gone with your love."

"I am the butter and wish to be on your bread, fresh and soft as it surrounds me."

"I love you."

"My innocence will feel at times like it is pagan. Still, the purity is love."

"Our blue is pavonian. As simple as a man in a field. As simple as a woman in a field. And as the season warms all things grow with harmony."

"A beautiful child will be born when the child comes. We will not question him, ever. He will be ready for us. We will see it in his eyes as he gazes into our futures. Trust much. Him. Us. He will see our love immediately."

"I love you."

"You will scan my troubled face and see my energy, and the way I am disturbed will be fine with you, and you will transmit your soothing hand upon me, and my smile will come when it is ready to come."

"We will see others with their eyes upon us seeking our gift, and our eyes will direct them to God."

"Love's joys will be in loving each other."

"Giddy, yes, we will be childlike, and in love."

"I love you."

"We will love each other for our virtue."

"Songs will be sung all around us. Perfect voices."

"You will wait on me. I will wait on you."

"It will be fact, we are one. Not just poetic words."

"Boldness will be with us. And sensuality is on us. Touching us as we touch each other. Aims will be our feelings in the combustible states of love making."

"I love you."

"We will always find time to speak to one another and express our love, our desires, our simplifications of togetherness."

"Our great love will be returned."

"The name of love will be our name."

"Our dreams will be love. All coming true as time lulls and then scoots us to the destination of our dreams."

"Getting along. We have the vital knowledge of that. We love one another as perfect as we can, and we celebrate that."

"Our love everywhere seems to magnify our lives."

"I love you."

"Truly and, at times, frivolously we will love one another."

"And love from me will grow, for you and others and for life both death and birth and rebirth."

"If I ever fail, I will tell you."

"I will tell you I love you."

"Your silence will be your charm."

"Yes, I love you."

"My secret culture for you will be all the time I give you to be you."

"We will be in love when we are together and when we are apart."

"You will be my fine imprisonment. I will cherish your bars because they will be made of the golden quality of love."

"Your heart, my glands are my total oneness inside you while your face points to me and smiles those love smiles. You have and will always have as time flows and I go and you go and come back a oneness together of nights in our bed become one and real and something gorgeous and we will not need food as we need each other's love and love will...

"I love you."

"Luxuries. In Buckeye we will live. In the house on Notre Dame. Love will flow. The community will better itself as we better ourselves."

"This ecstasy God gives."

"No wretched parts of love, only life and love as one."

"You will be out of sight at times but in sight of my soul, my soul for you. You will see it will remain pure for you. For you."

"Unique."

"I love you."

"Our wedding night, this night, like others, the charcoal of your figure in the warm, dark bedroom, the bursts of white streaming through our windows, I will stare at you, you me, we will be awake for hours, we will love each other, each to each, and we will feel fineness, the sad geometry of our bedroom will no longer mean a thing, no numbers but one and another soon, in a year or two or whenever God brings him, and I will reach a hand on top of your wonderful stomach and feel the boy coming, years away, yes, years away, and we will know more and more because we have love, sleepless thoughts, fingers groping for more and more love and it will be there for the fingers, fading rumbles, mouths mumbling, and far away as he is near God. God will multiply over us, and I will kiss, and you will, and the storm that started that night will be over, and quiet will ascend into our kindness, and life flows, the yearning will have stopped because we have each other, and words will be creative and gorgeous as love, and love, and love, and the night and love and the night and love and, finally, the day will break and love will brighten all over our souls, our souls, love, love, love...

The Axes: The Centers Of Rotations

*J*im and Jane have stepped beyond the love of kindness into the perfect realm of an honest, strong love. These are two whose worlds grow. Their brief rapprochement upon the living earth signaled their perfect affair with infinity. A world no one knew a thing about. One that was always called heaven. A minor word spoken too often to understand its meaning.

The two took long walks in Buckeye. Sometimes they even drove up to the lake to see Erie at sunset in the early spring. The flat horizon of the lake, the spring jumble of tiny leaves, and the warming sun setting across the huge town made Jim and Jane see life in a clearer way. The swish of green plants and the warm trees revealed their love growing quietly. The two were clearing chaos out of their lives. The two were seeing rhyme in the non-patterns of the vegetation. The trees horse thick or finger frail and the bastard tumble of the thicket near the smallest Great Lake allowed glances into the harmony of a God who does not easily reveal himself to regular people. But once love comes into lives, all things seem to magnify and to reach for a oneness that is not defined in words but in the harmony of the future. Sunspots brushed the couple's eyes and depicted a praise of their futures.

The disorganization of peculiar lives was ended. These two neat people were seeing a good thing happening. The disheveling of the past no longer upset them. The order of nature appeared on their sightscreens and they did not bother anymore to adjust the settings to see if they correct their lives. They were seeing that their lives were fine as one. The mystery of their fine gift was being understood. And that mystery pointed them into being non- starters. Now, the couple were just reactors to the good life.

Today, the sky was clear. Their marriage, the coming of a child, and the reasons for strength in their lives were making further understand the gift of good, good love. The quiet strength of the moment was deepening their hearts. As they walked along the big lake things were clearing for them. Yes, it was a will-to-do-good strength. Their manner was as even as a carpenter's level. Their humanity was growing to be as big as their benevolence. Their judgments were true. Their follow-up thoughts as persistent as the work of God. Both had grown a great patience about the rigors of life. Their love for each other was as soft as summer wishes. To be warm and secure, even the beauty of a night's breezes.

Their kind of friendship had become un-asking. Their loyalty to each was beyond even raising the subject ever again. Their tolerances of hardships on the job or with their families had become like Lincoln's. Deep, profound and lasting.

Their spirit for living was as hard as tempered steel. These two brought from them a measuring stick that brightly showed what true love was all about.

The two treated the earth with a simple benignity. They sat and watched the lake swell in the summer. Its beauty entered them, and they gave it nothing but smiles back. They bowed as a couple before the lake. The two were axes of love, for themselves, and for nature. The lake represented to them the preponderance of God and his doings.

It seemed clear to the two why they lived. Yes, they thought, love does this to all who were ever given the gift.

They seemed to want to ask humanity some questions:

Have you ever known sweet and perfect love? A love that is beautiful yet real and how it's almost impossible to express how you feel? A love that will last your time on earth and more? Love that is pure? Have heartache and pain have lessened it? Have you ever known a love that is always there and is never judging, and always fair? Have you looked upon a love that is as strong in your heart that nothing can tear it apart? A love that wipes away the tears, carries you through all your fears, and that is never criticizing; a love that defends you; that you can share all your desires with, your fantasies and your dreams? Have you ever felt a love that understands your innermost intimacies, a love that has survived the test of the years come and gone? This is a love that grows stronger as the years pass, a love that comes along once in a lifetime? Have you looked upon a love through the years that one has shared with you?

Jane said to Jim, "You are this kind of love; I love you. Thank you for being my sublime love!"

Jim and Jane sat in the sands of the beach with their little toes dug into the sand. On the horizon, at times, they felt like they could see way off the opposite shores of Canada. These times, that hillside above them felt like a massif, an immutable goal that was far away. Yet, at times like these, when their love was strong, it revealed a goal that was obtainable. The horizon revealed a thin heaven of warm shadows, like the flecks of a quail's handheld wings. Greasy Lake Erie was their boundary, but still, the heaven seemed reachable, and if all things were right, highly approachable. Death was becoming warm tints of reflecting sunshine. Before it was veiled. Now, it was alive with wonder as the two talked quietly to themselves about the venture. The wind stilled. Nothing collided on the opposite shore. All life was assuaged in the distance. The front in the future presented a perfect vagrancy from the hard ground of life. The two were feeling death's hard push, but the beautiful escape was becoming profound for them. Their wishes were a truthing. Jim and Jane knew that they would be traveling soon.

The axes were ascending. What was their turning point? Love. The world was becoming clear to them. Jim and Jane were figuring out that the world within their sphere had nothing to do with time, then they realized that world, that world of love, had everything to do with time, the immensity and intensity of time. Time was turning them into the one that a God yearns for those that are created. The steps to it seemed to be voluntary. Whether they were or not did not matter. The steps were being taken by the two.

Only a child needed to be born. Then, their endless, aquamarine journey would start.

Jim and Jane kissed, kissed lightly by the lake; the flat, massive and shallow Lake Erie. The depth of their kiss was beyond its sands. The loving spring evening was coming. There would be time for talk when talk called itself to them. Now, on their ride home their silence cast a deep glow over their personas. The oneness of love was blooming with the spring. The heat of their beings was making two lives worth the while. Meaningless time had quietly loomed in their lives. Now, it had meaning. A baby had started quietly kicking inside their lives.

Why should we get up in the morning? What do the questions mean, and why are they the right questions, but why do they always seem not to have the perfect answers? Jim and Jane have complete access to their source. They can read out the complete current state of their minds. No mental process is unconscious for them if they choose to perceive it. If somebody asks, "Why did they do that?", they can answer the question completely and fully. The ancient admonition of Socrates - know thyself - is fully and finally obeyed. But that's only half of the problem.

There are questions they intend to address. Their human minds weren't built, they grew - and they grew organically, haphazardly, and originally doing simple things in complex ways, starting from their immediate love instead of elementary principles. The human mind is an adaptation of its environment, not an attempt to create a correctness of the aging and dull earth.

Sometimes, you aren't sure what the outcome of a choice will be - it leads to several possibilities, which can be probable but aren't insured. Jim and Jane thought about many words, but also let the words come to them naturally instead of attacking them.

In this case, love, you try to pick the one with the most possibilities that best fulfills the most desires. Humans engage in love - taking a series of actions directed towards achieving a single goal. Of course, part of this is a natural consequence of a goal persisting over time; you use the goal to decide more than one choice. However, there are more complex plans ahead. To fulfill the goal of love, let it occur and do not worry over it. It will come. Just acknowledge love when it does. And cherish it. Being thankful that love has come to you. Jane and Jim did not put much time into complexities. They honestly just reacted to their feelings in the moment.

Formally, love is two calculations mathematically equivalent, although there might be a practical difference to the speed. One way of phrasing is sometimes easier to put into English, so we'll use the two formulations interchangeably. With all that fuzzy logic, the quantitative and algebraic versions handle the meaning of love a lot better. (They also provide a much richer handle for creating hope of eternity within the system, but unless you're an optimist, you probably don't care about that.) We're going to need the adoration system to get a feel for the subject.

Where does love usually come from? We haven't said anything about where hope comes from. Sure, love comes from super goals, but where do super goals come from? Or rather, where should super goals come from? Let's deal with the historical question first. The answer is love comes from being. Pretty simple? When we're born, evolution hands us love slowly: Survive. Eat. Reproduce through work. Rest when you're tired. Then, attract a spouse and fall in love. Take care of your child. Protect your nation. Act with honor (especially when you're in public). Defend your social position. Overthrow the bad stuff in life, and never let it take over your life. Learn the truth. Think. Et cetera (this is a big one because life has so many repeating things that occur). But do all this with a smile on your face because you have love inside your body and know that everything is fine because of it. You live everyday life, and, then, love falls your way and you do not realize its huge depth until you live more life with it in your grasp. Then, years pass, and you start to understand. And the little smile on your face become deeper and more lasting because you own something that provides you a gift that cannot be described. Sure, all the writers of songs and poems and stories have tried. But they have never truly described the feeling you have inside of your being. You are just smilingly happy it, love, is there.

Jane and Jim are saying that sweet emotions are worthy. They are just saying that they can all be right. They can all be true. They can blindly accept them as final justification. Granted that the reality of love exists, what do we mean when we say that a statement is "true"? After all, no absolute relationship exists between the words spoken and external reality. The couple can tell because it's possible to tell lies about love. This question comes courtesy of the really sharp doubters, people who assume nothing; people who doubt that adoration has any existence outside their own minds, people who, in fact, doubt the existence of their own minds, people who wonder if maybe the whole love deal came into existence a second ago complete with false memories.

Let's start with the quality of affection. These are the numbers of love. Another complex way to say one and one is two. And that is love. Jane and Jim felt the math.

What if it turns out that the meaning of love is something we build, rather than something we discover? Or what if turns out that there is no love, and it's all equally arbitrary? Well, in that case, you may as well go with whatever goals you feel represent your highest and best possible self; they'll be neither better, nor worse, than any other goals. Similarly, if adoration can be specified by the builder; or if there is no meaning, only goals; then whatever love minds build will if 'I could do that to arbitrary humans, I could do it to a rock.' The only way to force a rock to make correct choices is to use the actual truth logic leading up to the real meaning of life, whatever that is. I'm not that ambitious. All I want to do is find the choices that are, in fact, correct. The love.

The quail exists. You can doubt, but only by uncoupling a module from the reducible certainty of the loving animal, and even then, you'll still be certain that there is love. And you must find it immediately. And touch it. And feel its warmth. The bird flutters about. Watch it. If you wish to know love, you must feel the fluttering and then you will know its beauty.

Love Will End In A Cosmic State Of High Order

*J*ane considered math and thought the expressions are equivalent at times. The values of the indicators make love's reality a zed away. The equal sign promotes itself within the duo. As all numbers come into line, they sit for a while and then begin to oscillate. This humming is not visible. Yet, it produces a harmony among those feeling it. The opaque lighting transmits an alteration between the lovers. Love exists in this kind of math. Distant spaces begin to fade. Variables blur. Absorption into love makes the set of all numbers become a total. A band in space unites both right and left parts of the equation and a third is tempted to become beauty. The transparent reality of life pushes its head through the infinite space, all the results of love being totaled. Completeness prides itself within the scene as it sees lovemaking working. She smiles. He smiles. The third party this moment comes into being, tiny and living, and ready for the energy of love. Ready to grow. Ready to push itself upon the earth. Ready to be alive whenever he wishes to be alive. From an it to a him. When you are ready. He is ready. When he is ready you must be ready.

Forgiveness means an end to true debt. Jim and Jane in a union beyond foolish attempts to explain it. Sure trouble before union. Trouble afterwards. Trouble. Trouble. Still, love and child erase trouble quickly. Trouble is something that occurs between two after love is established as a oneness. Just like debt is. Just like buying a new car is. But, let's talk about trouble. In our society we make it a must. Why can't we brush over it and let it be and love each other? Why must everyone, the press included, emphasize it? Why can't we emphasize the beauty of life instead of belittling it with the awful hurts in the world?

The act of endearment is supreme. The act is supreme when the throttle is turned up. When there is more involved other than sex. Love and child and God. Exhilarating, so exhilarating that no truly meaningful words can be used to describe the excitement!

"I love you."

"Kiss you?

"You may."

"Time will stop."

"Our love has been waiting."

"Let it wait."

"We wish to make this more than love."

"Touch me."

"Your fingers, your fingers."

"Your smile."

"Your fingers."

"And now, your...your skin..."

"Touching you..."

"The warmth..."

"The spring..."

"May I kiss you?"

"Yes."

"Holding you..."

"Love..."

"I want you for all time..."

"I want you..."

"Do you hear God...?"

"I hear his hum..."

"I feel his beauty..."

"I feel you upon me..."

"Touching you..."

"And my eyes close..."

"And all is well..."

"You..."

"And you..."

"And our son..."

"Coming into being..."

"With love for him..."

"And us, and God..."

"I love, ah...ah...ah..."

"I love..."

"Oh God...!"

"Yes, I am, yes..."

"Love..."

"A son..."

"And us..."

"Always..."

A smaller God would not have brought the two love. Jim and Jane and a tiny boy feel God all the time. Fertility and each moment, a single moment that is convinced by answers to be real and true, and this tiny moment should never be disturbed by the wind. Here is where change should not ever take place. All was meant to be after love is fertile within. The seed is placed there. Many times, never fruitful...but this time, this first time with Jane and Jim, bearing the gift of true life. God's kingdom of time this one moment of truth.

The white-crowned sparrows are all around, slender and elegant and as active as nervous energy. There for a moment, then gone, then back. Migrating their energy in spring to bring its huge movement to Ohio. Up in little Buckeye, they are eying the dirty streets. Seeing the blooming of the bushes. And combustible life is all around. A nest. Another nest. An egg. Another and another. Warmth and tons of energy coming into life, being within life. Movement. The birds' handsome crowns show the purity of life when the vegetation is still mostly brown. Mating for life. One egg is hatched, then another, and another, and the feeding begins. All is well on the planet.

The two lovers create a vision, a little trick to share. It's quite simple, and it makes a big difference: The birds try to always have visions for where they want to go. The animals really try to think about life. "What do we want our lives to look like a year from now? Five years from now? Ten years from now? The day we die? And we try to do this for the projects we work on as well. For the places we are building. For pretty much everything we do."

Jane feels it doesn't have to be a complete, detailed vision. "I'm mostly visually and emotionally oriented, so for me it usually involves pictures in my mind, and how it feels to be there. It doesn't have to be completely accurate, but it absolutely must feel real and alive. And to make it come alive, it helps to have a lot of details. For me, it's a bit of a stretch to force myself to quantify the vision."

Jim argues, "By no means does it have to be a road map. It helps to have some vague idea of how to get there, but I don't want to limit myself to the products of my own meager imagination, when it comes to the steps, I need to take to get there. The best things in life are the ones that just happen, that you didn't plan for. So, I try to remain open, always letting the concrete steps of the path remain be in a little bit of flux, so I can change plans in an instant when serendipity hits. The only criterion is that it takes me in the direction I want to go. And since I have a vision, I have something to judge that by. When you don't have that vision, you procrastinate. You become a dull hum."

However, serendipity doesn't always help. Jane speaks,

"The vision, of course, changes over time. I learn something new about myself or about the world, and I realize that I no longer want what I once wanted. That's fine. Chances are that if I've based my vision on something real, my personality, my feelings, my idea of where I want to go won't change that dramatically. There'll be a lot of moments involved, because I don't fundamentally change all that much. I just learn more about who I really am. That I am an imaginary bird. We talk together in strong phrases, and, sometimes, we say things that should be recorded. But no one is around to record them." Two in love know more about the sciences than scientists. Learning should not come from those who are cold.

When you speak of love and all its attributes, letting it be spoken, yes, seriously and with reverence, but also some silly glee. Jane smiled after herself, and Jim made love. She began to laugh. Jim kissed and asked her what was on her mind.

"Glee!"

"You are silly, my love."

"You touching me means much."

"I feel I can do anything now. With you."

"You see. We are smiling. Life is fun."

"Life is, with you. And with our son on the way."

"Our love will keep us united."

"Yes."

"Yes, to many ways and to many things."

"Cheers to Love."

"And to you."

"And to you."

"And to him."

"And to HIM!"

The sky in Buckeye had turned peacock. The blue of the afternoon was showing itself. And all felt well and immensely alive.

Quanta In Mathematics Show Themselves Occasionally

I am Jimmy. I am within. I am old enough that I know it is time to get out. But I do not know how. I know I should just fight my way out. I do like to kick and squirm. Mom's been nice, but I got to roll. I will roll. Soon. Roll on the rug in the living room here on Notre Dame Street in Buckeye, then roll on the front lawn, roll around, and smile when they smile at me. Roll. And then creep and then crawl and walk, walk!

I am littler than little. I pee my white, short pants. Why do they call them diapers? I suck and suck. I smile at everyone. I am. A sucker.

I know lots of things. What I see mostly when I am outside is the sky. The other part of my life I live on. And both parts are big to me.

The earth is land and water. Wow, Lake Erie is big to me. That's all I know about. That is all that is needed. But I need Mom and Dad's love. Mostly Mom's. Yet, they are both nice. They know me. Well. I don't know them as well yet. I will soon. They sure seem nice. I smile when I look at them. I smile a lot.

I can eat crayons.

Everything is nice. Everyone smiles at me. That is all I know. I don't know about the news. All it is is pictures on the TV. I just know people making me giggle. Why do they always end up tickling me?

My room is good. My room don't drop, it's not a flop and sometimes my mom uses the mop on it. So there. Really am not a poet and I know it. Ha,ha,ha!

I like my dreams. They are short and sweet like me.

Animals like me. I like them. Why do they lick so much?

I liked heaven. I like earth. I will like heaven again. All three really is enough.

The moon is nice in the summer, even when it comes out during the day.

That big lake. That lake is an undreamed world, full of blue, and full of life that does not want to be seen. Its flat, flat surface hides a whole lot of beauty.

Mom took me to the beach. People laughed with me. On the blanket. Of course, they tickled me. They don't even know me, and they tickled me. Sun, and then Mom produced shade, and I could see better, and Mom hugged me the whole time, and that was good cause mom is good. She loves Dad. He's at work. Oh, now he's here, joining us with his smiles. Why is it when they look at me, they look at each other and smile? I think that's cute.

Water is good for me most of the time, but sometimes when it rains with cooler water drops my mom makes me wear a rubbery hood.

Waves are mostly just wrinkly on Lake Erie.

Life in water we can't see and feel sometimes. It's like sometimes life hides from us. I like water. I remember the warm water of little puddles in summer. It really felt good in it. Warm. It, the water, cuddled me for nine straight months. Wow, that was fun. And toasty. Do you understand why I really love my Mommy?

Mom washes my stuff with water, stuff in my room and stuff on my body, and the dirty stuff of my body.

I think the sun burns me, but I like its burn. It's like a Mom kind of warmth, but hotter. It's like creating life in me, like it does with greenie plants here in Ohio in the summer when beauty seems to be all around.

Yellow is our house. It, like the sun, welcomes us when we come home, welcomes us when we are home. Keeps us inside of it.

A lot of times I wish I was inside sun.

Now, I have friend. He likes sun. He is from next door. He smiles too. His Mom too. His Dad too. Lots of 'toos' in my massive world of fun.

The sun, the water, and jumping up, now crawling, now walking, and each day is new. Old people don't have anything really new except me.

I with Mom. I with Mom. I with Mom, ever. And Dad too. He is right next to us.

I am alone. Only at sleep.

Dad big. Mom regular.

I know love. I love. I smile.

What's in a bottle tastes good. Is it life?

I good. I am good. One day, be bad, but mostly good.

I look up see you two.

You smile.

You good, you really good when you see me.

I love you.

You me. That is enough. All I need. Infinite time. Infinite possibilities to do what I wish, as long as it's cute.

I want to tell you important things I know but I cannot speak. So, I will let a scientific kind of one speak. Here goes, but it is me. Trust me. Listen to me. Please. I know these things because I am a baby straight from God, and I will know a lot of things when I get really old. It's both of those times I know a lot, but in the middle times I only know a little bit of stuff. "There is infinite time. One would imagine that there would be infinite possibilities. Infinite time is probable. If one were to reach the speed of light, they would not age. If one were to reach the speed of light, symmetry would be broken, and the time would be broken. This would cause an endless amount of adoration, which would be somewhere throughout this un-measurable amount of time, allow all things to happen, ultimately breaking dull life, and creating a black hole in which multiple universes could be created. Parallel universes on which two or more share the same time yet are undifferentiated by space and gravitational pulls, which would cause one to orbit the other, mixing atoms and causing novas, black holes, and just like our sweet galaxy, would start an endless vicious cycle. That would sustain any thoughts. You would have such unbelievable thoughts. Yes, you would even understand a little bit of God because you would know a little bit about perfect. God, I like God!"

The day is over, to bed. Sleep.

See tomorrow. Night, I do not see, not see at all, except a night light, little light, little and big warmth all over house, and Mom and Dad check on me to see if sleep takes over me, and it did and that is fine, and it will take over for them, and that is good and they will smile at me when they see me tomorrow morning and that is good and all is good and all meant to be, and big God will come when I am ready to see big God, and that good too, and Mom will hug me and Dad will know that is good and I will go on, and on, and on... Boy, I feel good about being a boy.

Into The Blue Of The Sky
Is A Long Way To Jump

*J*im, Jane and time grew infinitesimally. After work they plied long walks in Cleveland, an innocent baby within their arms, marriage and time, and love ambling along. Everything was well in Buckeye, the poor side of Cleveland, on Notre Dame Avenue in the square state of Ohio. Jane was no longer working but taking care of their little life. The baby found sleep early in the night. The hours spent by the two speaking of days and love, and futures and love, and sweetness and time, and more love as a bobwhite quaffed and sung outside, singing a tale of himself. The summers were warm, falls cool, winter cold, and springs' sprightly temperatures found summers again. The birds in Buckeye were worth the watch. They rattled buildings, hugged the shoreline of the big city, and the people floating in their own history, not reading the Plain Dealer as much, but watching the news in their neighborhoods. A small covey of bobwhites chattered in the backyards. Windows opened listening to nature and God entwine.

The three wonders every night, rain or shine, went on their royal progress around the tiny town. Jane and Jim and miniscule Jimmy. Sometimes they would come home and prepare dinner and invite a friend or two over. The three were poor yet accomplished. They understood they were gifts beyond money. The simple dinner, and talk, and hugging and the little boy making quiet noises and hums about his perfect life on this Eden that was a simple planet. Offering constant hope to the three who already knew constant hope in the form of love. All this was happening as beautiful as beauty can be.

Sure, occasional sad blues wandered in, but on this day, a perse, a blue as solid as heaven floated its aura around the village. Giggles. Yet, death was a minute away. It always is, just as it is for all. But, until then let us smile, the three think. And they did. It's funny how people at peace seem to always have a smile on their faces.

And what is life after death? Are there words for it? Jim and Jane prepared to meet their maker in a garden as perfect as non-time. And here it is:

We briefly see what a final destiny is. God gave us a chance, like he does few others to see his true glory. An infinite quanta of math have been multiplied by themselves. The quantities of qualities are far beyond any quantities. When ether comes, and my God, there it is, an idea, a fathom, many good thoughts, and loving the sound of love, a warm love, trickling underneath and over more love. And there is God and he is knowing all and ladling huge breaths inside a loving couple; and all the impatience of within life is gone. All seasons are ended. One time, and then time itself becomes all knowing, and love and God and one, and the warmth of swelling sweetness as the high ground looks is all fine, and over and over a thanks is giving and you hear sounds from God like you were really loved all the time, and loving all is magnanimous, and few ministers told you all about all of this, and that is fine because you are here, here within a life that sits high and is not called a life, and worries, cares and tons are one below something you know nothing about anymore, and love in capital letters sings, and God and God, and God and God is not wondering if you desire God, and then God is coming to you and staring, staring a lot, and sliding into your lips not a worry in this massive village, and over and over the summer no longer has negatives and so forth and so on and on and on, and your tongue and your life is feeling so right, and all this is garnering all the energy, and music is playing over and over and quiet lyrics are rejoicing, and blue and blue and no contrasts exists, and sands and sands of good seems like skies and skies of wholesome realms of glory, and a good and a steady sky expands, and clearness and kindness and no coming rains and the branches of times spread into this infinity that welcomes you, and welcomes and quiets when you wish, and singing with you both becomes a wonderful future, and in less and less verbs time stops, and you do not feel it flying and all good and good is all and all good, and your child is fine on earth, and earth's a good stepping sound and good is a good stepping stone, and you feel the meanings like a second coming, a good one, and all the lips and lingering and caressing in an uplift, and no torrents, and your mind is a nonentity, and calmness of eons and so on and so on, and all casual walks and the overcast of good and searching steps collide in a solemn ritual that is right for once, a wonderful yawn comes to you, and clean, clean ultimate love, and no more foolish TV dramas, and nothing to wait for, and nothing to worry over, and you sit and ponder a good time and are thankful, so thankful.

"I see a scroll. And on that tablet, I see a perfect figure coming into view, and I am happy and you are happy. Oh, my love, when will this figure arrive?" And Jane says, "Yes, the figure is in a tunic, and there is the pallium and a scroll. The left hand is soft and perfect. And there is a large tree. And this tree has a wonderful aroma."

"A right hand is stretched out towards us and we are not afraid because we have experienced love and that is fine as fine can be, and we are ready for any trip we have with God." Jane speaks, "A naked figure, and that is glorious. Other fine trees are a long way away and they seem to be searching through a mountain pass. Nothing divides us. We see adoration after knowing love."

"All is right." Jane, "All around is healing and good. The birds in the trees sing melodies that are different but have a unifying harmony. This scene is all like a kind of baptism. This one scene is beyond earth glories."

"I see you, and you smile with one that is deep and lasting."

"And that is all I need to do in this new world."

"No nude demonics. A healing we are going through that is lovely. And a glorious love." Jane, "Glory, like we are getting a fragment of fragrant heaven and knowing all will be well."

"Yes."

"Yes."

"My near-death experience opened the world to me. It made me think about God and other dimensions that are in life, which I had always known, but did not admit. I feel the insanity of all ambulances as they rush us through the evil streets to a hospital. Years have passed since my underground life with death. Am I dying, I said? Am I outside myself? I see my body and its enduring love for me. I look all my heart; it seems pale and lifeless. My life cannot move. My face is white. I am glad it is over, and that I have love. I watch as the walls of the hospital dissolve. I see the lights of the town speed toward me. I can see the moon! What am I doing up high? Why does everything look small? Memories pass before my mind as in a movie. I see family at the foot of the bed and am amazed at why they are there. Suddenly, they are gone. From where they stood, I see folks rushing toward me with unknowing speed. They race toward my open arms, expanding then falling apart. Face after face flies over me! I am in wonder. I'm drifting. I'm unable to keep my eyes open. Who are these events all about? Some of the wonders I recognize as God telling me answers I've known that have died years ago. Others I do not recognize. Where is my life? There it is, and my life has made me be prepared. Now the whole room is filled with God! He hovers near me and looks into my eyes. I try to push him away. I fight him. The experience seems to go on forever. These are spirits who are restless. Their faces are twisted with pain. They seem lost. It's frightening to see him walking back and forth around my bed. And now – God with his glowing face comes close to me. He reflects a gentle and powerful light, reminding me of the pictures of beautiful angels that I love. I feel nurtured and loved by him and enveloped by his perfect luminescence. This true being is made of light, and even though his brilliance is intense, I am not blinded. Tremendous compassionate love surrounds me! He is filled with the essence of love and compassion. This magnetically glorious power is filling every atom of me. I have never experienced such depth and power of love. Now, I see the power of love merging into an intimate dance where all boundaries have disappeared. I feel myself one with this being of swift moving compassion. No words or sounds are being exchanged, and yet total communication is happening. The strong presence assures me, 'Yes, you are understanding me, and all the beginnings and endings with me now and you are not worrying. To me you are being born. Do not fear a drop of life. I have eternity waiting. You have always been with me; I have always been with you. I know you. You just fell asleep during your time of maturity, and you are awaking and forgot momentarily who you are. Now you are remembering.'"

"This was knowing and meeting him in an instant. His revelation fills and nurtures me. I am a being of light and I am of him! What is this surge of atomically thrilling energy? It began as a gentle vibration rising through the length of my body, from my feet to the top of my head, but now my whole self is vibrating. I hear buzzing. It is growing louder, and now the vibration and the buzzing are becoming with the one, and with me. I am in love; I am understanding good love; I am his compassion! My presence now fills the room. And now I feel my presence in every room in life, and in death. I am realizing they are both one like the one who is directing me. Even the tiniest space is filled with this presence that is him. I sense myself beyond life above the city, even encompassing earth. I am melting into the universe. I am everywhere at once. I see pulsing light everywhere. Such a loving presence envelops me! I feel I am now one with God. And I am glad."

What was is what is. What is is what was. What is is what is going to be. There exists less words, more time, and then, no time, and ever a last word. And many on earth forget all the foolish things they once had to remember. Some remember and that is fine, and then, they leave, and memories are goners, and that is fine, fine indeed.

This Scene Shows Age, Youth, And Death As Unified

*T*he unity was a blue that spoke of heaven in a liquid way. A perse hue. The love, the wedding, the pastor, the two, the love, the family, the love, a child now a toddler, and the parents leaving, and smiling, and the love. They kissed, they loved, and then, they died. The love and eternity became a huge unity. Yes, a pastor's tragic words, but the love. The love.

Definitions and distinctions are forms of closure. The primary form of math within lives is not injunction but description. Wittgenstein said, "...whereof one cannot speak, thereof one must be silent." The mathematician was speaking of two formed into one. He was trying to say that mathematicians say nothing.

Musicians do the same. Both play their instruments. And this is all anyone can do. Play.

Bertrand Russell wrote, "What causes hesitation is the fact that, after all, Mr. Wittgenstein manages to say a good deal about what cannot be said, thus suggesting to the skeptical reader the possibly there may be some loophole through a hierarchy of languages or by some other exit." Math dies too. Math dies to live its eternal life. Jim and Jane are wholesome math, and they equal love for each other and for the oneness. The unity of crisp marriage was together in a meeting place beyond words or math or breathing.

Let these two be forms distinct away from life. God must have said this. Yet, not many listen. Many do not reach for ultimate love.

God says without speaking in his usual whisper, "Let the mark of those distinctions be one. No individuals are in heaven. From one form I create them into a heavenly universal form, a meandering of their spirits into one perfect whole. This is my kind of love. A love they were set up to know when they were alive and within a human's love. I have an even better love in heaven. A better, perfect love comes. This love has come to them."

The pastor prays and prays. He knows this is his only job and it is a good one. He says, "Let there be an indescribable kind of time. A time that drops the perpendicular and finds hard trust in God is good. Call heaven one-and-one-and-one and let it be the way it was intended. No crying. Let the crossing be in peace to a state of being that is indicated by a token, a simple token. All is condensed here. All has power. The glory of non-language in heaven. The glory of your majesty, dear Lord. Ah, sweet Jesus. Sweet Jesus. Your gift is beyond any accurate description."

Doubly meaningful is this death. The two. Jim and Jane.

A nameless reporter might write, "These two mandatory primates find peace. No more rattling sounds for them. The clicking of earth's life is now a hum. The primitive has become the complex, and Jim and Jane are enjoying themselves in a realm that stops words from getting in. Heaven is a math, a marking on finality. No more brackets, no more indicators, no more infinity because the two now are within this awesome word and once two are there, there is no need to discuss the concept. The concept is real and beyond real in an instant."

Jim and Jane feel like Vikings as they visit. But they do not want to go home. They want to go on further. Such are Jim and Jane within their, endless home.

The two are blind animals, able only to distinguish the inside from the outside. Huge space, an exploration of smiles, a distinguished form, multiple circles in an inch of warm time. Einstein knew there was a place where time came to a crawl. But, did he know there was a place where time did not matter?

Jim and Jane. All their lives they wished to draw a distinction. Love was coming for a long while, and then, love came and they did, now, death, and the final distinction. All their senses have nothing to do with this distinction. Death is beyond the senses. They feel what Spencer Brown felt when he said, "If only we knew that every even number greater than two could be represented as a sum of two prime numbers." Now, Jim and Jane understand many things without speaking about them. Yes, God knows all, but now the two know more than three. They know more knowledge that exists on earth.

The covert has become overt.

They have been cleaved from earth but not divided. They are distinguished in this indivisible state. A math that involves God's love.

Mathematics is done for now. Jane and Jim are beyond simple numbers.

We know we must die. Do the animals? Jane and Jim had talked about this before their passing into the dream kingdom. After their many words, they knew there was no answer in the here and now. Now, they know they have the wonderful answer.

The two did not live through death. Freud thought death was abstract and negative. What did he know? The lovers found out the psychologist knew little. He did not know that you begin to die, you begin to be. This is what the two had said and found there was truth in the words. No one on earth listened to the lovers. Such is the case when you speak the truth on earth. The death instinctively had crawled within them for the years they were in love. And now it was final and good.

Jim and Jane used to talk to each other as the baby nursed. They thought in their own way that the present state of death that most know is oppressive in society, and maybe it should be so that folks can understand the beauty once they pass over. They wished to picture themselves in a beautiful black forest, surrounded by thousands of coniferous trees. A spider cries as he swings from tree to web. He is singing in a tone no human can hear. This moment is the wonder of it all. Jim reached out and picked a cone. He closed his eyes as Jane looked into it. Jim heard a crackling sound behind him and turned to see a bright red cardinal break a twig in his beak. A tree grows, and Jane does not hear it, and a tree dies, and Jim does not hear it. As the two leaned down to smell the fragrance of the earth, a tree frog stares down at them with wide eyes, as he clings to the bark with his webbed feet. Suddenly the sky lightens, and it begins to rain. The two reached out and plucked a huge leaf from a bush and held it over their unified head for a tiny umbrella. The cool rain falls on the surface of the leaf and drips off the tip, and onto them. As Jim and Jane begin walking to their new home, a snake slithers across their path. No, this is not an imaginary place. It is a tip of life they have been missing. Life has existed for millions of years upon Jim and Jane's single earth, and it is the only place this exists in the vast universe, and they know this and that is fine. NASA will find nothing in the eons that follow the two. What space explorers are looking for is here and only here.

God's leer throws a Jack card into the hardcore group of the aged in their homes in our society. He sees the non-truths hidden behind the con of growing old. The aged rattle around a bit, but mostly stay quiet until death. After they die, they realize their words were just tremors on a still globe. The aged look at their father and say little. They know he is like Jeopardy, full of answers that no one knows the questions to. All watch but no one can care. God's answers do not consist of deep, overt hope. God's answers will never be heard by people not listening for the answers.

There is more about love and death. More. When? Whenever. Despite its popularity in humanity's field of experience, the word death is rarely defined. There are many references to its causes and effects, but a simple definition apparently escapes most people. To this end God offers one. Relating on a higher level. To understand the meaning of this definition, the supreme being has to first define the words "relating" and "higher level". By relating,

God is implying two entities and a mutual comprehension between them. By higher level, God means a level of integration beyond the three-dimensional world based on the few senses the living possess. Putting these two things together brings us to a more verbose definition, which can be stated as follows; death is the mutual interrelationship of two entities on a level of integration beyond our three-dimensional world.

The next point to consider is the implication of a precise definition of death. Assuming the definition God has presented is right, what practical considerations does it imply? One obvious one is to separate love from it, which should be understood as two separate things. Love can exist without death, and death can exist without love. Accepting the definition would clarify and rarify one of the most muddled, subjective areas of the human condition. Using the definition, God can conclude that the death act has the potential to emotionally focus the vague, indefinable feelings that it causes between two people. Likewise, two people within death can use love to celebrate their mutual relationship, although it's not necessary if the two people have a high enough level of consciousness. The opposite implication of the definition is that any three-dimensional, selfish use of love for personal ego gratification cannot be rationalized or qualified by calling it death.

Another practical implication of God's definition is the ability to sort out the jumble of emotional states between entities that are usually lumped into the generic use of the word death. Any appreciation of something on a higher level that cannot reciprocate in kind should properly be considered adoration, the deepest form of love. From an esoteric perspective, this definition implies a more profound respect for what death is, as relating and understanding on higher levels is what esoteric philosophy is dedicated to accomplishing. God feels that the conclusion to be drawn from all this in an esoteric sense is that death is another way to gain consciousness once you know how to apply the psychically powerful energy it contains.

Two Can No Longer Hear
The Physics Of Life

A wave of grief, sadness, and anger washed over life in Buckeye. Without warning. The sadness was suddenly being consumed by dulled sensations. Burning tears ran down cheeks. It became difficult for many to breathe. The grief gasped for air, as it stood transfixed in the old roadbeds of the town. To this day it could not tell how much time transpired, but as these feelings, this emotional overload passed, it found itself exhausted as if it had run a marathon. Crawling up the steep embankments of the homely place to get out of the road, the hurt turned and looked back. It was a bit shaken, to say the least, and wondered at what had just taken place. Life was difficult getting back to what it was because it felt so weak. Death in the real world does not have any answers, just questions. It would one day receive answers, but not until more than an eon later, and then, from a most unusual source. With great energy men and women labored to save life. They called on each other to pray to God, and sometimes he is not to be found. Or maybe he is so subtle, no one can see his answers. Men and women labored as earnestly and bravely to see the reasons as they did to save the love these two possessed. Answers about death come slowly. But they do come with faith. They do come. One must just listen.

Two love, two loved for years, two love again. Such are the workings of a God who has infinite gifts.

Jim and Jane know that you wish details. The human race wishes to know all the answers. Jane and Jim meandered into their bliss. And stayed there. Permanently. Death, the real leveler in life, stays, and so did love for the two.

Some would say premature death visited Jim and Jane. They were just getting used to love, a child, and the future of serene sweetness in Buckeye.

Some would say it is terribly romantic. Death came after the making of their love. The beauty and drive of a perfect climax seemed a bit jilted by the word that has a reputation of such utter demise. Both, as one, their incredible feelings coming as one, the huge breaths, the total love behind their thrusts into life, in front of and around the two magnifying their timing, and their eyes peering into the eyes of God and showing the warmth of total devotion. But then came their infinite sleep. Yes, the slow breaths came to both. Then, the finality of entering another vista came to the lovers. The only equivalent on earth is two looking out from a massive mountain and seeing the Eden that is earth flowing away from them, and then, knowing peace without the speaking of any words. A world God had set up that was beyond words that accurately describe it. And the child, sleeping in his crib, two years young, and not knowing, not having any understanding of this magical world his parents had entered, and waking at his steady time in the morning, eight am. And the father-in-law unlocking, coming in the front door, coming to baby-sit, as he did every morning of the work week, showing love, so that his daughter could fix the house up and do some shopping. Yes, he put his key in the door, opening it, coming in and saying his usual hi, and hearing no answers. Never panicking, looking to see if the boy was fine, and he was still half-sleeping and wriggling in his crib. Then checking on his daughter and seeing two lying in bed quietly. Noticing they were not breathing. And understanding, because he had dreamed about this happening to his wife and him someday, that death had come. And the true and only ultimate peace had arrived. Funny how he understood right then, right at that moment, that all was fine. Yes, if he had walked in and seen Jane making breakfast or heard Jim showering, he would have also felt things were fine. Very fine.

Premature death, or was it? The big either or. God knows such things. God does such things. God would answer to the right or wrong of these things. Give God time. Take a deep breath and give God time to show everyone how to think about such things.

Two extraordinary people had a mission in which they were supposed to fulfill. When they accomplished it, they were no longer needed on this grand earth, for providence had used them, used them for something. Byron, Mozart, and Raphael had passed on early, their work done. The world was created to last a long while and God's timing is not measurable. All was in-sync. All were happy in Jim and Jane and their multi-talented worlds. There would be light cast on their ignorance, and on others' questioning. Give God time. Time. And there would be light cast on their wonderful talents as waiters of magnificence. Because whether it is a Mozart sonata or a little boy, both are tender gifts.

The death? The death. Death. Yes. Scary to us who are alive. But it is nothing to those dead. We living, as we live, death is not with us. Just a thought, yes, a terrible thought, but just an idiotic idea God has dropped on us to signify time. We exist, it (yes, death) is over there. Then, it comes and we do not exist and do not worry over it. Death has a peace. Think about it, does life? We realize it is not an exclamation point, just a dull journey into another realm, one we have picked, if we pick God. Jane and Jim were combined in a blissful empyrean. They had made good choices on the dangling earth.

Jim and Jane knew you did not live through death, that it was not an event of life, that it was a separate realm. Visual fields are with limit. Death would prove that to the two. For death is beyond limit. To these two, death had become the discreet and dignified exit to a Zion's kingdom. The two were finding that death was tall and clear and cut from a God whose eyes looked straight ahead and sparkled. A God who was slim and powerful and un-speaking because of the weight he was carrying. An aura of light surrounded him, and that light was sound and clean and honest and directly shining into their eyes, so quietly. For these two who were kind of quiet in their everyday lives.

Death is sharp. And you are drawn to its persona. If all your sheep are in line and you are ready. Death is old, but when you get there, you feel young because its eyes point you in a direction that is endless and reassuring.

This great law of us sentient beings is enforced by a God who seems to flip through us like all the cards in a deck. You are made to go. You go, and if you are ready all is calm and you feel like a cool jello, alive and ready to be downed with a sweet aftertaste. This is the utmost limit to a final gasp of a breath. And death liberates you from even the thought of evil. Heaven is a clean kingdom, a Paradiso, a docile utopia, a rhapsody, a rapture, an ecstasy, a transport into the seventh brevity of longevity. And it is awfully interesting. In life, death and the sun should not be stared upon. When Jim and Jane came to the kingdom, they stared a terribly long time and did not move, as in forever.

Before the two left in bed that evening, Jim was speaking of death, "I wonder if death is life?" Jane answered softly, "I do not know."

"I do not know either. I know I love you. I hope God finds that enough. I hope he finds that I love my son, that that is fine. I hope."

"We should pray. O God, give each of us his and her own death. A death that mirrors the lives you have given us. The blessings, a good son, a good place to live, and a good house to live in."

"Praise God for whatever God gives us. He has been good to us three people."

"God gave us meaning, love, and need. And that was more than fine. I cry when I think of how our maker came into all our lives. I am shedding good tears."

"Let us sleep on that dear. Close your eyes and rest, rest."

"Yes, sleep fine. And let our son sleep well and awaken to a new world that God gives him."

"We should close our eyes." The two went as one into an everlasting bedrock of repose.

Death is a feeling and everything more. Some pain when birth comes. There is some pain for those and others when death comes. It can be a kind of aching. A steadfast love pulls all parties through the climaxes. Then a great feeling arrives. The feeling gives you thoughts to look forward to. The whole process is a comeuppance.

The climax is gradual, like sleep. It happens and you know it is happening, and then, deep peace is brought on and everything seems over and begun at once. And all of it is just becoming. No languor. Just like babies, who are not aware of when they passed into the threshold of life. One is not aware when they pass the threshold of death.

To cool a burning life, death comes. So thought Jim years ago. And here it was. Here was a man for the first time finding himself feeling the leer of the eyes of death and finding out it was not worth worrying over. The truth was now commonplace to him. His spirit was entwined in the long question, and it felt the responses' calmness. Jim had passed through the rare moment, and he found it was almost trivial. His vision, no, it was not small. His learning, no, it was brilliant to an extreme. And the ultimate feeling, no, it was huge beyond the meaning of the entire earth because it involved a place where time was nil. His feeling was of the immense waters of the earth deep and blue. His burning tongue had been cooled. He felt he was deeper into the mind of death and all seemed to be getting more well as time passed. And as time passed, time became nonsense.

Jane became one, but not alone. Like love and Jim and life, all had melted into a holy cream. The river of death flowed along calmly for Jane. She had the wondrous feeling Jim was along for the eonic ride. Manifold agreeable aromas flowed with them. The music they sensed was the music they longed for their entire lives. The forty odd years, the shortness of their lives meant little to them at this time. Jane felt a smile about it all. The flowers of death were all over their garden. The length of love perched upon their souls. The non-look at long life perfected in a meld of warm and smooth cream. The delights of their delivery molded their passing. The roundness of heaven's river rocked their movements. Yes, there was warmth in the waters and wonder in the watch of their non-worries. The golden sand of being saved was on the beaches. Jane felt no longer the jostles of jagged life. She was now touching the tastiness of non-time.

Jim and Jane heard a great voice slumber them in a few hearty words, "The preparation of time for you was planned. Behold God's holiness. This is a church of infinite wisdom." Then a moment that was timeless came and another gazing voice said, "I dwell with you."

The gates to his voice were pearls. The streets had become a clean gold. And the shining light was not that of the sun, but of the wonder of God and his non-time. And the two were saved.

In the freeness of time is a better period of lasting and everlasting. No enslavement, and more pleasures than good work. Nature is not a great part of this nation. Still, earth was good preparation for this place. No power truly existed, but God was exclusive. The energies of attainment were the happiness on earth.

Inexhaustible sources of pleasure were in this non-time. Substances were only the highest of ideas. The constant hope flushed within of the rotation of complete fruition.

No novelties consumed these two. The frequencies of their accommodations were sweet ideas. A most exquisite source of pleasure donned on them the power to love as one infinitely. The minds became as fruitful as an orchard in spring. The newness of results was endless. And Jane and Jim had satiated interests in the gratifications of successions. From moment to moment, they felt deep inside the journey of sweet love. Benevolence associated with total interest in ever fostering numberless instances of liberation. Oh, such the prosperity of non-prosperity. Music held onto them. All was warm, all was feeling like they have been fed, all was content with non-life and the music kept playing, playing at a volume that needed no clicks.

Blades of grass need not grow. The leaves become a feeling of the place.

A unified singularity possessed nothing except all the realms of wonderful thought. There was no need for moral law. Or law at all. And the music kept playing. Like all on earth was a preparation for total goodness in the non-weather of complete heaven.

Comfort was provided, and so was all the wants of philosophers. Double qualities of forever gleaned the two habituating the bursts of their virtues. Ample room for the most equal of people fluttered into this glory. A securing of the boundlessness of wishing lives brewed. The best architecture of complete humans donned the holy psalms.

No eulogies needed, most of the ones on earth forgotten anyway.

The industriousness of non-work bloomed. A non-ever but it had an all-encompassing love that ever lived on earth.

Victory with non-loss was all around.

The self was no more; the one was no more. The truth before the one had done the work, and now, the truth did not need to be thought of. Cum deo. But not needing God was the sign of the time.

In a paradise luminous flowers encircle like choirs in a perfect song. Infinite degrees of abstraction make it all beyond the sweet beauty of the earth. Massive threads of muscles tightening and loosening surround around the waste of time. This concludes in a pneuma. The miracles, the floods of goodness grasp at slingers of wonderful memories. The sirens singing is such the gift and produces wings like violins in music. Jim and Jane had left every hope behind, for all enduring hope was here. Amusement, the non-work of amusement abounded in the deep conjoining of rhythms. Laughter alone began smiling within the template. A word who would sooner sleep, and he did, and he did. So, this paradise did not tempt one. This Paradiso was one.

Being lay apologists, like all humans, Jim and Jane gazed without words for an ever that seemed brief. Their spiritual bodies entwined as one. They became stars of the landmarks of love. Their future was existing at this moment. Their son was calm at his early age to know all this, and never fear a God and his ambitions. Such is the purity of babies on the earth. They knew God better than wordy, earthly adults, even pastors. Sadness is in the age, and as one got older one had to endure it. On earth, the bountiful earth, there are some things one has to always deal with as life rolls by.

All communication here in heaven is through thoughts. Jim, "The secret delight here is the security, the permanence of goodness."

Jane, "We are protected from speech, our minds flowing. Our love increased."

Jim, "I love thee more than the beauty we had on earth."

Jane, "Yes, and you, you are beautiful."

Jim, "The knowledge, the preciseness of the non-words I feel. Ah, your sweetness. And God's."

Jane, "I am satisfied with the symbolism of each moment. And you."

Jim, "Everything here begins. Always."

Jane, "Everything is together."

Jim, "I feel white as a sheet, and I cannot see myself. I cannot speak to you with my mouth. I can dream of perfect dreams and they come true. I wish to know God further, and I believe He will come to me at his own time. Ah, the love of the non-place, the non-time!"

Jane, "And me too. We paid a price for our ways on earth. But look at the fruition. Marvelous!"

Jim, "The endless site. The sight within God's hearing. Our souls, our oneness, our love; and no time!"

Above the non-horizon a bank of clouds divided and became silver within gray. Far out upon the non-ocean a non-ship was stationed in constant non-movement. Jim and Jane gazed at the swelling sails.

They felt they had led direct lives, good lives, and that they had done good things in the midst of a rhapsodic God. That they did not live lives in vain. That the earth grew because of them and that they had had a piece of perfect love, and that that had been their destiny. They thought and thought. They had transcended death and were now in permanent passiveness, and that their gift, God, would take their futures and bring them ultimate love.

A letter to the parents:

Our Dears,

If you knew how death and love take turns crowning God's achievements, you would not worry another moment.

We know how you love each other. We wish to try to tell you the meaning of love. That it is beyond earth. That it is God's magnificent gift. That it is the blossoms of heaven. Wholly joyous you will be. All for of you.

Sensual is death to those who love, love deeply beyond the minor gift of sex. We wish to console you in this prayer, relieve you of your burdens so you may look forward to the ultimate day. Exceedingly dear is time. We know that now. This better is a best world. We are the love of angels. We send you an adieu that never ends.

Love, Jim and Jane

Jim turned abruptly toward the waters. And continued his smile. He said to right to himself, "I do not know what I did yesterday because there was no yesterday. The sexton of my ship removes me from worrying over pitiful things. I am stayed here. When I see God's face, I will ask him tons of questions and He will respond the way He wishes to respond, and all will be fine. I will never blow on his embers in this ship. I am his sailor, his deed doer. I am happy. I am not ashamed to pray to him. I feel his comfort. I feel his non-time. The eons I do not and will never fear, never ever will fear. Will go on as He directs, in his goodness and flowing glory."

Jane spoke, "No doubts now. All is extraordinary since death. No musings about absent persons. I am with God and Jim in that order, and all is fine as fine can be. My musings are all positive, all full. Hours are more than seconds of memories. Non-time is taking over my life away from earth. And that is how it was meant. Nothing has perished. Fullness is within. The sea, always calming and detailed as I wish it, is here and is everywhere. Our love affair is a veritable liaison of hope. Remoteness is inside of this millisecond. I love all. I love God. I am with my sweet, sweet Jim."

Last Words

We, to the end, are made. There are occasional blues. The colors are wondrous. We are Jim and Jane. We are with ever. And the beauty we feel is any simple golden flower you view. The intense brightness falls from the air, and the light makes us see the heavens. The natural vision is the way. Gold is the light in the future of the mind. The flower opens the mind even as ones pass. Strength and faith had stooped inside our grave and brought us here. Yes, here, and the words are few to make you who are living understand our deaths. Whatever time, do not worry over. Whatever time has passed is fine, fine. Now, everything is still. All is cyanosed, in that blue tint, and there is God. And with God the other attachment is love. God mostly is hard to understand. Love is not. The passion it creates stays. In the end, please ask God to help you find love, find it in the blue that is the cloudless sky. Love, soothing as the warmth of the blue of that summer sky we met, met in dreams and created the love that is the honey of the eternal flame. The delight. Ah, the sweet caress, the caress, the enduring caress of wondrous love.

CPSIA information can be obtained
at www.ICGtesting.com
Printed in the USA
FFHW010628281019
55746985-61613FF

9 781612 447728